**"I have a proposition for you..."**

Penny looked at Will, trying to read his expression, but in the flickering light of the fire that wasn't easy.

"I'm listening."

"I have a theory about relationships that has served me well most of my adult life. It's that the maximum time for them is two weeks."

"Go on."

"There's something I want to make sure of first."

He put his arm around her shoulder, drew her closer. Their eyes met and held and she couldn't look away.

Whatever he meant by two weeks, she wanted to know more. His breath brushed over her lips as he exhaled, and he lowered his head slowly, giving her a chance to retreat...but she didn't want to back away.

She wanted his kiss.

She wanted to forget the old Penny and be this new, exciting woman...

Dear Reader,

Merry Christmas! I'm a total maniac this time of the year. I've made my children dress in Santa hats and matching sweaters and pose with our dog (also in a matching sweater) all in pursuit of the perfect picture to capture our holiday. And to be honest that's sort of what drives Penny to go away for Christmas. Her mom is out of town with her newish husband for the holiday and the thought of staying home by herself doesn't appeal. She's lost her joy and needs to recapture it. She's sort of figured out how to do it when she meets fellow holiday-escapee Will.

Will has found a way to enjoy life in short bits of time and his ideas sound good to Penny, who is tired of trying to get everything perfect in the big picture. I had so much fun writing this book and bringing to life all the cute holiday snow festivities that I, as a Florida girl, never experienced. If I could, I'd make Penny and Will dress in matching sweaters and snap a picture to add to my holiday album.

Happy reading!
*Katherine*

# *Under the Mistletoe*

---

***Katherine Garbera***

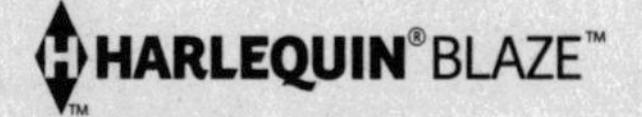

ISBN-13: 978-0-373-79830-8

Under the Mistletoe



This edition published by arrangement with Harlequin Books S.A.

For questions and comments about the quality of this book, please contact us at CustomerService@Harlequin.com.

**Printed in U.S.A.**

**Katherine Garbera** is a *USA TODAY* bestselling author of more than fifty books and has always believed in happy endings. She lives in England with her husband, children and their pampered pet, Godiva. Visit Katherine on the web at katherinegarbera.com, or catch up with her on Facebook and Twitter.

## Books by Katherine Garbera

### Harlequin Blaze

*One More Kiss*
*Sizzle*

**_Holiday Heat_**

*In Too Close*

### Harlequin Desire

*Reunited...With Child*
*The Rebel Tycoon Returns*

**_Matchmakers, Inc._**

*Ready for Her Close-up*
*A Case of Kiss and Tell*
*Calling All the Shots*

**_Baby Business_**

*His Instant Heir*
*Bound by a Child*
*For Her Son's Sake*

Visit www.katherinegarbera.com for more titles.

Other titles by this author available in ebook format.

Family and tradition define every moment of my Christmas holidays, so this book is dedicated to Charlotte and David Smith, who raised me to love the season and to never forget the reason for it. Also to my grandmothers, who are no longer with us but whom I miss more keenly at Christmas, Rose Wilkinson and Priscilla Tromblay.

# 1

PENNY DEVLIN HAD decided that she was giving herself an early Christmas present this year. A vacation from her life. Actually, making herself not read another email her former boss and ex-lover sent her was the best gift she could ever really give herself.

He'd made a mockery of her dreams of a white knight and cost her a job she loved. Rat bastard.

But really, who would keep working for a man like him?

Not her. Mentally she gave herself a pat on the back. She'd made the tough but right choice to leave her position as an event planner at Papillion Clothiers, and this place was her reward.

A ski chalet to herself for fifteen days at the luxurious Lars Usten Lodge in Park City, Utah. Her phone pinged again. She groaned as another text appeared on her screen from Butch—or actually from the label she'd assigned him.

JerkButtFace: Stop being a baby. I need to talk to you.

Penny: All my files are in my former office. You don't need me.

JerkButtFace: Not about work.

Penny: All we had was work.

JerkButtFace: Stop acting like I did something wrong. This is the 21st century.

Penny: Jerk is the same now as it's always been.

JerkButtFace: Name calling? You must still care.

As if. He was so frustrating. She *didn't* care, and was coming to realize she hadn't ever really loved him. That was the worst part.

Her phone pinged again.

*That's it!*

She flung open the front door of her very lovely, secluded alpine cabin, stopped to admire the gently falling snow and then chucked her cell phone out the front door.

"Hey!"

She glanced up just in time to see a man batting away her cell phone before it fell to the ground. She'd almost hit him in the face.

*And what a face.* A strong, square jaw with just the right hint of stubble, firm masculine lips curled in a sort of sneer, and bright, Chris Pine–blue eyes. He wore a heavy shearling jacket and a pair of faded blue jeans that clung to his thick, muscular thighs. His boots were covered in snow, and as she let her gaze travel back up his body, she forgot why she'd been so fuming mad just a second earlier.

"Sorry. I'm so sorry! I just couldn't take my phone one more second." She knew that sounded totally lame, but it was the only thing she could think of other than: *Yowza! Hot guy alert!*

He chuckled. The sound was deep and rich and echoed in the silent snow-covered land around them. It was cold, and the air seeped through the fabric of her chic lounge sweater, but she wasn't tempted at all to go back inside.

Full disclosure? This guy was the perfect distraction. He held a leather suitcase in one hand and a brochure from the Lodge in the other, so she assumed he had to be a guest. She glanced at his left hand to see if he was single, but he wore leather gloves. Plus some married men didn't wear their rings all the time. "I've been tempted to ditch my phone more than once," he said with a smile. "What seems to be the problem?"

"Problem?"

"I'm assuming part of the technology isn't working," he said.

He sounded logical and normal. All the things she just didn't feel right now. And he was cute. Really, really cute. So if she played her cards right, perhaps she'd be able to salvage this and flirt with him. She wanted to. Needed to reclaim a part of herself she'd lost when she'd learned the horrible truth from Butch. No denying it.

"Um…it wasn't picking up the Wi-Fi," Penny stammered, making up the very first thing that came to mind.

He bent over to pick up her phone. Seeing him holding her pink, jewel-studded case in his manly hands made her feel funny. But when he glanced over at her with those piercing blue eyes of his again, she still couldn't help but stare back. This time she noticed he had sun lines around his face. He spent a good deal of time outdoors, she figured.

"Mind if I give it a try?" he asked.

"Sure," she said. He was a really good-looking man with his thick brown hair styled to one side so just a swoop of it fell over his forehead. No way could his hair be as soft as it looked, but she wanted to touch it and find out.

He glanced at her screen and then back at her.

"It seems to be working. You've got a text from… JerkButtFace. Apparently, he's desperate to explain."

She groaned. When he said it, the name sounded… well, still funny to her.

Of course, even though Butch was married and his wife was pregnant with their child—something he'd failed to mention when they first met or at any point during their six months together—he still expected her to be his girlfriend. Something that she definitely didn't want to hear him try to justify again.

And he'd still managed to wriggle his way between Penny and the first attractive man she'd met in months. *Ugh.*

"I know. He's like a broken record."

"I take it you've heard enough?" the man asked wryly.

"You've got that right. But watch out, I seem to be a moron magnet," she said, moving out of her doorway to approach the man. Her UGG boots protected her against the snowy path as she did so.

He smiled at her and shook his head as he handed her phone to her. She put it in the pocket of her long lounge sweater.

"Will Spalding," he said, holding out his hand.

"Penelope Devlin." She took his hand to shake it. She worked in the business world and probably shook hands at least three times a day with potential clients, so she was used to weak ones and even clammy ones.

But his hand was smooth and dry as he enfolded her fingers in his, and the grip was firm, but sort of gentle, too. He looked to be in his early thirties, close to her own age. She stared at their joined hands for a moment as a tingle spread up her arm. She pulled hers back and then looked up at him again.

"You are a very interesting woman," he murmured.

She was not sure how to take that. "Not really. I get very boring once you get to know me."

"I highly doubt that," he said. Her phone beeped from her pocket and he raised one eyebrow.

"I'm sorry I almost hit you with the phone. I was aiming for the snowbank."

"Why don't you just put it on silent mode?" he asked.

"That would have been logical, but I'm afraid I was pushed beyond that," she admitted, hoping he didn't think she was crazy, but already suspecting that her first impression hadn't gone very well. "I know it's a sickness, really, but I'm waiting for an important work call."

She'd applied for another job with a big, high-end New York retail chain. And they were making the decision this week on who would get the position of senior event planner. If she got the job, she'd be in charge of the company's parties for the various fashion weeks around the world.

"See, to me…that part is logical. I can't ever really detach from work, either," he said, giving her a half grin that made him even sexier. "That makes you even more intriguing…"

"And mysterious? I've always wanted to be mysterious," she declared.

She liked the image he had of her. She could be that woman. Right now, she could be any woman she wanted to be. She was free of everything. A man who'd been way too secretive, a job that had been demanding and had that awful perk of working for Butch…

But that was behind her now. Will thought she was intriguing instead of old reliable Penny. That would be very exciting and different.

She'd be able to enjoy her holiday the way she'd planned. She thought of the framed print that she'd propped up in the kitchenette of her cabin.

*No Regrets. Just Good Times, Love, Peace and Lots of Chocolate.*

Will Spalding seemed the perfect man for that if he was single and interested, and she acknowledged there was a 50/50 chance he wasn't even single. Well, he *looked* interested. God, what if he was another loser? Granted, a very sexy-looking one, but still…

He didn't look like a loser, though. Not with that firm square jaw and serious expression on his face. He looked like someone who lived life on his own terms.

"I'll leave you to the snowbank. I look forward to seeing you again," he said.

He continued walking down the path and all she could do was watch him go. He had a seriously nice ass.

She didn't realize she was staring until he turned to the cabin next to hers and then put his key in the lock and looked back at her. She shook her head and waved and then dashed back into her own cabin.

He was cute and she felt incredibly attracted to him,

and for thirty seconds she just stood there letting all those feelings wash over her. She even felt a bit like her old self again.

Wild. Free. And ready for adventure.

WILL HAD BEEN on his own since he was fourteen. He didn't say that to gain sympathy, as he was a trust-fund baby used to having whatever he wanted—as long as it was something that could be purchased. And for the better part of the year being alone suited him just fine.

But Christmas was his Achilles' heel. He hated not sharing it with someone else. Christmas brought with it lonely memories that he had learned a long time ago would overwhelm him if he didn't ensure he was distracted.

Being a man of action, he'd developed a very simple way of dealing with it: affairs that lasted two weeks. That was the optimal amount of time. Plenty of days for fun and not enough time to form a real bond with another person. One week left him wanting more, and after two weeks the novelty was gone. No strings, no hurt feelings afterward, just two weeks of pure, frivolous pleasure for him and the lady of his choice.

He'd learned that the hard way during his brief marriage when he was younger, and had decided to limit himself to just two weeks.

Will put his leather suitcase in the corner and thought of Ms. Penelope Devlin next door. On the surface she seemed like his favorite kind of distraction.

She was cute and funny and a bit charming in her awkwardness. He'd been very good at keeping his affairs light and making sure the women he got involved with wanted exactly what he did from the affair—fun and temporary companionship.

Penny was definitely intriguing. Maybe she was looking for something to take her mind off her problems. Plus that one innocent little touch of their hands had shaken him to his core.

It had been a while since he'd felt the zing of lust at first sight. And he wasn't sure he was ready to write it off simply because she might be more than what he'd been expecting to find. Ah, hell, who was he kidding? He wanted her. And unless she shut him down, he was going to go after her. No bones about it.

Which made her dangerous, because he was simply looking for a casual affair, not a woman who could touch him all the way to his soul.

Shoving those troubling notions aside, he unpacked, checked his email and then realized that he totally sucked at relaxing when he glanced up and realized the sun had already set.

Where had the time gone?

He could eat dinner in his bungalow…but he'd be alone with just his thoughts, so he put on his shearling coat and snow boots and left his cabin. He stood in the doorway and looked at the night sky, so big and bright on this clear, cold evening. In the distance he saw the twinkling of lights down in the valley where the town was.

His breath puffed out in front of him as he locked the door and went down the path leading back to the main lodge. He glanced at Penelope's door as he passed it. Someone had hung a Christmas wreath on it and strung some lights around the door frame. It looked homey and festive and not at all like his dark doorway.

"It's beginning to look at lot like Christmas," he muttered aloud.

It was just the little nudge he needed to start thinking more about Penelope. Maybe she was just what *he* needed this Christmas.

The path to the Lodge was lit with gas-style electric lamps with holly wrapped around the posts. A light snow was still falling and he promised himself that tomorrow he'd take advantage of the ski slopes. But that left a solid twelve hours to fill and even though he had international business interests, he didn't want to spend the entire time working.

He climbed the steps that lead to the lobby past the lounge area that was dotted with fire pits and large padded chairs. There were families roasting marshmallows and couples snuggling under heavy blankets, and he just kept walking into the building away from all that…togetherness.

A blast of yuletide music hit him as he entered the lobby. "Last Christmas"…it had been his mom's favorite song. Funny that he could still remember details like that, but not her face without the help of a picture.

He paused for a moment to listen to the song and let those faraway memories wash over him. There were times when he wished for things that couldn't be. He shook himself and walked straight to the bar and ordered a seltzer water with a twist of lime. Though what he really wanted was a double shot of whiskey neat. Being a recovering alcoholic was a constant struggle.

But he'd never been good with self-control, especially when he felt like this. Truth was, he'd been unable to describe this feeling to any of his therapists, and there had been a lot of them during his teenage years. He just knew when he felt this way, he could destroy things—including himself—and not give a crap.

But the last time he'd done that, it had taken a lot of time and money to clean up the mess, and he still had some scars from that incident that hadn't fully healed.

"Gin and tonic?" Penelope asked as she slid onto the seat next to his at the bar. She'd changed out of those leggings and the long sweater into a micro-miniskirt that ended at the top of her thighs, and her furry boots had been replaced with a leather pair that hugged her calves. She looked chic and fashionable.

And drop-dead gorgeous.

She wasn't tall but sort of average sized and curvy. Her blond hair was pulled back around her face but left to hang free. It was stick-straight and looked like sunshine to him. She'd put on some kind of lip gloss that made her mouth seem full and kissable.

*Kissable?* Really? Was he going to be the kind of sap who—

He knew he shouldn't stare at her legs and forced his gaze to her face. But the image of those long, shapely calves lingered in his mind. He wanted to reach down and put his hand on her leg but that was too bold. Even in this mood.

Her eyes were a welcoming shade of blue. Different from his own, darker and more exotic.

"Just tonic, unfortunately," he said. He waved the bartender over and ordered a gin and tonic for her.

"Did you get your phone sorted out?" he asked after a long moment.

"Yes. I figured out how to block him for now," Penelope said, chewing her lush bottom lip. "So are you married or engaged?"

He shook his head. "No. You?"

"Would I have someone labeled JBF if I was?" she asked.

He laughed, because he suspected she wanted him to, and he'd also noticed that people talked more when they felt at ease. Plus, he'd been told one too many times that his face could be intimidating when he wasn't smiling.

"I guess not."

She took a sip of her gin and tonic and leaned in toward him.

"Feeling really adventurous?" he asked, because despite the fact that his gut was saying it was a mistake to get to know this woman better, he wanted to. He wanted to know if her hair was as silky as it looked and if her skin was as soft. He wanted to know if she'd be as fun in bed as she was out of it.

She arched one eyebrow at him and gave him a wink. "What'd you have in mind?"

"Something daring and dangerous—dinner with a total stranger."

She tipped her head to the side. "That *is* really risky."

"Why do you say that?"

"Well, you never know what I might do or say if you stick around."

"Like I said, you're a very interesting woman, Penelope Devlin."

She nodded coyly. "Yes, I've decided I am. And I will have dinner with you."

"Good. Now, how adventurous are you? Will you have a private meal with me in my cabin, or is it the hotel restaurant for us?"

"I'm not stupid," she said. "We have just met so I'll take the hotel."

He smiled. “Perfectly understandable. Would a picnic dinner by one of the fire pits work for your comfort level?”

“Yes,” she said, taking out her phone.

“What are you doing?”

“Texting my friend, who is the general manager of this lodge, to get the scoop on you,” she said.

He reached over and put his hand on top of hers. “I’ll give you the full rundown while we are eating. You did say you were ready for an adventure…”

She nodded again but it seemed more for herself than for him. “I guess you’re taking just as big a risk. After all, you know I’m armed and dangerous.”

She held up her cell phone and he chuckled.

“Yes, you are,” he said. She fascinated him; there was no denying it. The more he got to know her the more he wanted to be around her. There was something about her smile and her body… Hell, there was no denying he wanted *her*. This was Christmas, after all, so why shouldn’t he make it the best one possible?

# 2

WILL LEFT HER to go and make plans for their dinner, and asked her to be on the back patio in thirty minutes. She stood alone in the bar with her gin and tonic, thinking about life. She was excellent in a business situation. Give her an event for groups from fifty to a thousand to plan and she was in her element, but put her one-on-one with a guy—a smoking-hot guy—and she froze.

"You look like you are contemplating something serious," Elizabeth Anders said as she slid onto the bar stool that Will had just vacated.

"I am," she said.

"Why?" Her best friend had a more relaxed aura now that she was engaged to their college chum Bradley. The two of them had been friends forever, and over Thanksgiving had finally given into the steaming sexual tension that the rest of the world had always seen between them. Now they were madly in love and planning their life together.

She hitched in a breath. "Well, you know how I'm supposed to be giving myself Christmas this year?"

"You know I do," Elizabeth said, signaling the bartender and ordering herself a Drambuie.

"You're off the clock?"

"I am. Bradley and I are going for a moonlight snowshoeing walk as soon as he gets here."

"That's nice. I'm so happy for you." And she was. Truly. But she was also jealous. She wanted that kind of romance in her life.

Usually she was too busy with work to think about that kind of thing, but Will was making all those fantasies she'd tucked away for someday seem like a possibility.

"I got the idea from that photo you'd posted on Pinterest of the couple walking in the snow."

"No fair stealing my romantic fantasies." Penny pouted.

"I thought one of us should take advantage of it. Plus you are better at romance than I am." Elizabeth's blue-green eyes sparkled. "Bradley loved the idea." She smiled at her friend and then reached over and hugged her. Normally Elizabeth was all business so she struggled to make small talk and be social outside the corporate world but lately she'd been trying to change.

"I met a guy this afternoon," she said, picking up where she'd left off.

"You did? That's great! Where did you meet him? Why isn't he here?"

"I kind of tossed my phone out of the cabin and almost hit him in the head."

"Nice. I guess that's why he's not here," Elizabeth said with a grin.

"You'd think, but no. He said I'm *interesting*. We're

having dinner in thirty minutes. A picnic on the patio by one of the fire rings."

"You are? Who is he?"

"Will Spalding. He's staying in the cabin next to mine. Do you know anything else about him?"

Elizabeth withdrew for a second but Penny didn't mind. She knew her friend was using her razor-sharp mind to search for details about Will. "Last Christmas he stayed at the Caribbean resort that Lars owns. He always books in for two weeks at the holidays, and he's due to check out on New Year's Eve." She grinned at her friend. "I can pull up some info about him if you want? I know he asked for a Christmas tree to be delivered on the twenty-first and that's about it."

"That's okay. He's going to give me the scoop when we have dinner," Penny said.

Elizabeth gave her an incredulous look. "Yeah, sure he is. He's probably going to tell you whatever he thinks you want to hear."

"I'm pretty sure my bullshit meter is more than ready to weed out his lies," Penny said. "He's my holiday fantasy. And unless he is a complete troll at dinner, I think I've found my distraction."

"Really?"

"Uh-huh."

"Then why did you look so serious before?" Elizabeth prodded.

"It sucks having a best friend who calls you on the BS."

Elizabeth laughed. "Yes, it does. So what's up?"

"I like him, Lizzie. He's funny and charming, and I think he could be a lot of fun. But given what just happened with Butch, I'm afraid to just let myself relax and enjoy it, you know?"

"I do know. But I also know that you aren't going to let him slip away. If you want him for Christmas, then make him yours," she said.

"My own Christmas hottie?"

"Definitely."

"Should I be jealous?" Bradley asked, coming up behind Elizabeth.

"No," Elizabeth said. "You're my hottie."

"And you're mine," he said, bending to give his fiancée a kiss.

"And that's my cue to go," Penny said, downing the rest of her drink. She was happy for them and everything, but she might have misjudged coming here with them so happy and in love. It made her wistful. Made her wish she had some kind of radar that would help her steer clear of losers. "Have fun on your walk."

"We will," Bradley said with a wink. "Where are you heading off to?"

"Dinner with a tall, dark stranger..." Penny replied.

"Go, Penny!" Elizabeth said, holding her hand up for a high five.

She gave her one, walking out of the bar. She wanted to believe that this was simply dinner and nothing more. Will Spalding didn't have to be anything other than who he was. She needed fun and uncomplicated. A Christmas gift to herself before she had to make some serious decisions about her future.

WILL HAD NO problems ordering the dinner he wanted for himself and Penny. The concierge was more than happy to secure a fire pit for them away from the families roasting marshmallows and singing carols.

Christmas lingered in his mind like a festering wound. Probably because it was the one time of the year that it really hit home that his family was gone and he was alone. He tended to wallow in it, starting around Thanksgiving. One year before he'd finally gotten sober, he'd spent the entire month of December drunk.

"Is that all, Mr. Spalding?"

"I'd like to do something after we eat. Any suggestions?"

"We have a horse-drawn sleigh that I can reserve for you. Our guide will take you on a path out toward the ski lifts. It's scenic and on a clear night like tonight it should be beautiful."

"Sounds perfect," Will murmured. "Is the gift shop still open?"

"Yes, sir, until nine."

"Thank you," he said, turning to walk away. He went to the exclusive, high-end women's boutique that was tucked off the main lobby. He found a Scottish-wool scarf that had the colors of Penny's eyes and had it wrapped up, and asked the sales girl to send it to the concierge with instructions to have it in the sleigh later.

These kind of romantic gestures he'd learned early on. Women appreciated them and he found that a happier woman made for a more enjoyable evening. And money had never been an obstacle for him. He knew the gift was small, but he also had realized pretty early on that it was the small things that mattered most in life.

And he wanted Penny. Wanted two weeks alone with the pretty blonde. He headed back to the bar and noticed her high-fiving her friends.

Maybe he was kidding himself by thinking she would agree to a two-week Christmas romance. Despite her throwing her phone earlier, she seemed like someone who was a bit healthier in relationships than he was.

He doubted she'd need anything from him. After all, it wouldn't be the first time he'd misjudged someone. But this time he hoped he was wrong. Because, more than anything, he wanted her to need him so he could focus on making her Christmas special and ignore the gnawing emptiness that he still felt deep inside. She pushed off the stool and turned to walk toward him. He watched the way she moved. Her hips swaying with each step she took. Her breasts bouncing the slightest bit. The effortless grace that was arresting to behold. He realized he was staring but didn't care. Penny smiled when she noticed him watching her, and for the first time since he'd started thinking about Christmas, he felt lighter. He didn't care if nothing else came of this evening than dinner in a pretty woman's company. For tonight that was enough.

He didn't have to think of the past or the bruises he always pretended weren't there. He could just enjoy this evening with a sweet, uncomplicated woman. Someone who could make him forget the truth of who he was.

"Ready?" she asked, coming up to him.

"I am. Are you going to be warm enough?"

"I think so. If not, you can keep me warm," she said with a wink.

"I can?"

"Unless you don't want to, but then that's the whole point of inviting me to dinner, right?"

"Indeed. Let's go." He nodded toward the bar. "Were those your friends?"

"Yes. They just got together so they are still kind of too cutesy each time they see each other."

"Too cutesy? I don't know what that means," he said.

"Kissy and huggy. Wow, now that I said it out loud, I really do sound jealous."

"I'll hug and kiss you if it makes you feel better," he drawled. "I believe in giving a lady what she wants."

"You're quite the white knight."

"What can I say? It's fun to make another person happy," he replied.

She slipped her hand into his. "Dinner is a good place to start."

He led the way to the semisecluded area where his name was on a chalkboard under the word *RESERVED*. They had a thick, camel-colored blanket on the padded bench and the fire was roaring. There were thick potted pine trees placed around the area with brightly colored Christmas lights on them.

Will gestured to the bench and she walked over and sat down on it. Joining her on the comfy seat, he draped the blanket over both of their laps. He saw one of the waitstaff standing discreetly out of the way and signaled the man to bring their meal.

As the food and a table were arranged in front of them, he stretched his arm behind her on the bench and leaned in. The clean floral scent of her perfume surrounded him. He closed his eyes, reminded of a spring day in the mountains near his home in California.

"I didn't ask if you had any dietary needs," he said.

"None," she admitted. "Healthy as a horse."

She shook her head and covered her mouth with one hand. "Maybe this would be more romantic if I didn't talk."

"Not at all. I like hearing you talk. So you think this is romantic?"

She gave him a sardonic look. "As if you didn't know. Yes, any woman worth her salt would think this was romantic."

"What's the problem then?" he asked, because there was definitely something more going on here.

"Just me being me. When I'm in a setting like this, I want to be perfect and all the ways that I'm not seem to make me stumble. I'm sorry… I want to be the glamorous sort of girl who'd fit right in here, but I'm going to say dumb things."

"No, you're not," he said softly.

"Trust me—I am."

"Honey, you're going to say things that are going to show me who you really are." Turning toward her, he stared into her captivating blue eyes. "Besides, I'm not interested in someone who is pretending to be perfect."

PENNY ENJOYED THE dinner that Will had ordered. It was just a smorgasbord of meats and cheese and artisanal breads from the Park City Bakery. But what made the dinner so lovely was Will. He was funny and urbane. Obviously well-traveled and cultured.

Being with him made her realize how lacking Butch had been in those departments. He put her at ease. Made her feel like it was okay to be herself. And for the first time since she'd learned Butch was married, she felt a spark of hope.

"You look very determined," Will said as he finished off the last of a cheese straw.

"Do I? I was hoping to look intriguing," she said with a self-deprecating laugh.

"It's hard when you keep laughing. Femme fatales don't laugh," he said.

"They don't? I've met a few spies and they do laugh," she said.

"Do they? How do you know they were spies? Maybe they were just pretending," he said.

"I wouldn't be surprised if they were. My mom is a lobbyist so I've met all kinds of people in DC. Speaking of which…what do you do? You haven't said."

"Sorry to say, I'm not a spy. In fact, I'm in commodities, so not even a really exciting job."

"I don't know that that means. Are you a trader?"

"More of a speculative investor. Commodities are things so I invest in things, not in people or ideas."

"Interesting," she said, still having no idea what he did.

He laughed. "I spend a lot of time on the internet doing research and reading company profiles before deciding if I should invest in them and their products."

"Is it profitable?"

"Usually," he said. "What do you do?"

"I'm sort of between jobs at the moment. I was the senior event planner for Papillion Clothiers," she said.

"Interesting," he said with a half grin.

She arched a brow. "Don't tell me you don't know what that is."

"I've heard of Papillion and I know what an event planner does, but I'm struggling to put the two together."

"Mostly I plan events around the various fashion weeks for our high-end clients," she said.

He glanced at her curiously. "Do you like it?"

"I love it. Clothes and parties, what more could a girl ask for?"

"Truly? Is that all it takes to make you happy?" he asked quietly.

Suddenly, she didn't feel like being light and pretending everything was perfect, but she knew she had to keep up the charade. No matter that he made her feel like it was okay to be herself. The past had taught her it wasn't. "Most days. Especially at work. It's a world I enjoy and I like getting paid for it."

"But in your personal life?"

"I like clothes and parties in that, too, but that's not all I need to be happy," she told him.

"What is?"

"I think defining happiness isn't a first-date subject," she said evasively.

"Is that so?" He leaned in closer and the scent of his spicy aftershave surrounded her. "As far as I'm concerned, there's not a better time."

"Why?"

"Because we don't know each other well enough to put up barriers. Right now there is just potential and we can be as honest with each other as we want to be."

"Okay, then. What makes *you* happy?" she asked. "If you want to do this, then you can go first."

"Touché," he said.

"It's harder than you thought it would be, isn't it?"

"Not at all. I'm just not all that into happiness. I'm more a contentment sort of guy," he replied.

"Really? Why is that?"

Will shrugged his broad shoulders and gave her an inscrutable look. "Happiness is a chimera. Something shimmering in the distance that most of us keep striving toward but never really reach. But contentment is easier. I mean, right now I've had a nice dinner with a very beautiful woman in front of a roaring fire. Nothing could be simpler than that."

Penny thought about what he'd said. There was more truth to it than she wanted there to be. He'd been honest and now she had to be, too. She owed it to the man who saw happiness dancing just out of his reach to stop pretending to be something she wasn't. Ultimately, she knew that she couldn't make another person happy. She never had been able to do it and doubted that in this moment with this man it would be any different. Contentment was all he was aiming for and she suspected she could manage at least that, but a part of her wanted more.

"I don't know if I buy into that. I've been truly happy at times, usually with my friends when I can let my guard down and be myself," she admitted.

"Are you being yourself now?" he asked softly.

"I am. Coming off a bad relationship makes it so clear to me that I can't stomach lies," she said.

Then wished she hadn't.

"I can't, either," he admitted. "Which is why I have a proposition for you."

She looked at him, trying to read the expression in his blue eyes, but in the flickering light of the fire that wasn't easy.

"I'm listening."

He rubbed his chin and gave her a rueful grin. "Don't take this the wrong way."

"Um...if you keep hedging, I'm not going to have much of a choice."

"I have a theory that has served me well most of my adult life about relationships and it's that the maximum time for them is two weeks."

"Two weeks?" Great. Sounded like he was another

guy who wasn't for her. But at least he was being honest. "Go on."

"Before I do, there is something I want to make sure of first."

He put his arm around her shoulder. Drew her closer to him, and she let him. Given that this might be their one and only date, she wanted to go for it.

Their eyes met and held, and she couldn't look away from his intense blue eyes and the expression in them. Whatever he meant by two weeks she wanted to know more. His breath brushed over her lips as he exhaled and he lowered his head slowly, giving her a chance to retreat, but she didn't want to back away.

She wanted his kiss. But she needed some answers first.

# 3

Penny put her hand on his jaw and felt the stubble of his five o'clock shadow. She liked the way it abraded her fingertips and she sighed.

"Sex. That's what you're proposing, isn't it?" she asked, withdrawing her hand from him and getting to her feet.

Penny shivered a little bit from the cold but stood her ground. She'd never been wishy-washy in her life. Even with her bad relationships, she'd gone into them with her eyes open.

"No. I'm talking about the fact that we both know we're going home in two weeks. It would be silly to pretend we didn't."

"Go on, I'm listening," she said as her teeth chattered.

She got back under the blanket and he tucked it around her. He smiled at her—it was tentative and roguishly charming, and she had to smile back. "The next two weeks, leading up to Christmas and then New Year's Eve, we spend together. We do all the things that couples do and we enjoy it."

She nodded, trying to be analytical about it, to treat

Will as if he were a businessman pitching an idea to her. "What's the catch?"

"That we both know it ends on New Year's Eve. That this is just temporary. To pretend this could be anything else is a lie."

She thought about it. She'd had her fill of lies that were told to her by men. "So you're proposing a vacation fling?"

"No, a Christmas affair…a sort of gift to each other," he said. "Unless you're not interested in me."

"I almost kissed you," she reminded him.

"The almost is the part that I'm concerned about," he said, frowning slightly.

"You kind of said you had a proposition for me. I needed to see what you meant before I took this any further." She hitched in a breath. "But for the sake of argument, why not try to make this into something real? Don't you believe in love at first sight?" she asked. "I know not everyone does, but some people do."

He rubbed the back of his neck and reached for his drink, taking a couple of swallows before looking her in the eyes. She knew stalling when she saw it.

"No lies," she said. "That's my rule if we even consider doing this. I don't care if it will hurt my feelings or if it's too raw for you. I will not tolerate any falsehoods."

"I think there is a story there," he said wryly.

"You haven't convinced me you should hear it yet," she retorted. "But it involves Jerk Butt Face."

He laughed. "I am not good at relationships. Courtship and romance I can do—no problem—but the heavy-duty lifetime-together crap, not so much."

She arched her eyebrow at him. "Might have something to do with the fact that you call it crap."

"Might be. But experience has taught me two weeks is my maximum," he said.

She wanted to know more about that but didn't push. He offered her something temporary. "You're proposing that we just both go into this with our eyes open. Have a great time and keep it light?"

It seemed almost too good to be true, but she was tempted. She needed something to make her remember all the things she loved about her life. And all the things she liked about being with a man.

Before Butch had come along and made her feel nothing but bitter resentment… "Yes," he said. "That's precisely what I'm looking for. But I'll understand if this isn't for you. Not everyone is good at compartmentalizing."

"I take it you are?" she asked.

"I am. But as you said, we don't know each other well enough to go into all that."

"The nice thing about what you're offering is that we don't have to. I don't have to try to make you into the man of my dreams."

"No, but I wouldn't mind being the man of your *fantasies*." His voice dropped a seductive notch. "I find that when women and men are too focused on making 'it' work, they lose out on experiencing all the things they truly want."

Boy, was that the truth. She hadn't been too pushy with Butch because he was her boss, but also because he had seemed like a nice normal guy. She'd called that wrong.

"Can I have some time to think about it?" she asked, biting her lip.

"You can, but we only have two weeks," he reminded her. "So don't take too long."

That was true. But— No, no buts, she thought. Thinking and weighing the pros and cons had netted her a holiday by herself. The gift she'd really wanted was a sexy man to share it with. Will was offering her that very thing.

It was only her fear that was keeping her from leaping into it. She didn't want to make another mistake. Who did?

"I have arranged for a little surprise for you," he said, breaking into her thoughts. "Why don't you think it over and meet me in the lobby under the mistletoe in thirty minutes if you're interested."

"What kind of surprise?" she asked, but she already realized that she liked his surprises.

"An outdoor one, so you might want to get changed," he said.

"What if I don't show up?" Penny asked. She tried to imagine him standing there waiting for her. No guy she'd dated in the past would have done that, would have left themselves so obviously open to being stood up. "Won't you feel silly standing there?"

"Not at all. I'll feel like a man who missed out on knowing a very special woman. I hope you'll take the chance and let me make this a Christmas we can both remember."

PENNY WASN'T TOO sure about Will or letting herself know him any better. Two weeks sounded fun in theory, but the truth was that she wasn't always supersmart when it came to love. She fell for all those losers and the sweet promises they made—but seldom kept—because inside she desperately wanted to be loved.

She knew it. Her therapist had confirmed it. And let's face it, all those bad boyfriends over the years had just reinforced it.

But Will was different. He wasn't making her any promises. All he'd said was, *Let's be each other's Christmas present. Meet under the mistletoe to accept.* And now she stood in the corner of the Lodge's big reception area, waiting to see if he was going to show up.

She'd taken her time with her hair and makeup, wore a pair of slim-fitting black pants and a cream-colored silk top that showed off her curves. She looked her best. But now she just had to believe in herself. That was part of why she kept falling for those guys who couldn't give her what she needed.

But believing in herself in a relationship was always a slippery slope.

"Hello, gorgeous," Will said, coming up behind her.

She flushed and turned toward him. A few snowflakes still clung to his thick brown hair, and his bangs fell forward, brushing his face. His blue eyes were bright, but she noticed that he was watching her carefully.

He wore dark jeans and an olive green sweater that accentuated his muscular physique and broad shoulders. A few snowflakes still clung to his thick brown hair and his bangs fell forward, brushing his face.

"Hello." She reached up on the premise of brushing the snow away but really just wanted to touch his hair.

"Are you waiting for me? Or hiding?"

"Neither," she said. "Just giving myself a swift mental kick in the attitude."

"Why is that?" he asked.

“I’m not sure about you yet, Will. I don’t have a good track record with men—something we’ve discussed. And I have to be honest here, you are almost too good to be true.”

“A sort of Christmas miracle?”

She had to laugh at the way he said it. He had enough confidence for both of them.

“I haven’t decided yet. You could be a mean old Jack Frost just blowing chilly air and leaving ice in your path.”

He gave her an enigmatic look as he peered down at her. “I have no way to prove I’m not. But we both know the girl who threw her phone in the snowbank wants to take a chance on me. So I’m going to go stand under that mistletoe and wait.”

He walked away, his stride long and confident, those jeans still hugging his butt. Trans-Siberian Orchestra’s “Christmas Canon” played in the background and Penny stood there, hesitating for a second before she realized that she wanted Will. Wanted him enough that she was going to go for it.

He’d said two weeks was the optimum time to just enjoy each other, and she was going to just have to take him at his word. Besides, Will seemed like the perfect sort of Christmas surprise that she couldn’t *wait* to unwrap.

She walked slowly toward him, the music dipping and swelling, the scent of the large pine Christmas tree in the lobby filling the air. Her courage and her hope were building with each step.

She stopped right in front of him and he gave her a cocky grin. “Knew you couldn’t resist me.”

“Maybe I just felt bad for you standing all alone under the mistletoe,” she said, leaning in to kiss him.

His mouth was soft and firm as his lips moved under hers. With their breaths mingling together, sheer physical need inundated her senses. She felt the tip of his tongue brush against her lips, then gently part them. Shivers ran down her spine until she forgot everything except this man. Will.

He put his hands on her waist to draw her closer, but she broke the kiss and stepped back. Just because she'd decided to take a chance on him didn't mean she was going to lose her head. She was going to keep her attraction to him under control.

"What was that?"

"A kiss," she said.

"A pity kiss? I expected more from you," he said.

"You're going to have to show me a little more of the man who thinks two weeks is enough time to get to know someone."

"Fair enough. I have a surprise for you," he said, sliding his hands up her back and pulling her into his arms for a more thorough kiss. He took his time with it and she was struck with how good he tasted. It wasn't just the fresh taste of his mouthwash; it was more than that. Something that seemed to stem entirely from Will.

He angled his head to the side and thrust his tongue deeper. She lifted her hands and framed his face with them. Spread her fingers over his five-o'clock shadow and then drew back.

"Where's this surprise?" she asked, even though she wanted to pull him into a nice private corner and have her way with him. Keep kissing him until they were both so turned on that they could forget about everything except each other.

"Outside. Did you bring a coat?"

"I did," she said.

She'd left it at the coat check and they walked over to get both of their coats. Then he led her out the door, which led to the ski slopes and outdoor area with fire pits and trails. A chill wind blew a light snow around them as they walked. Her neck was cold and she wished she'd brought a hat with her, but she'd forsaken it for vanity's sake—so her hair would look good.

Warm sounded better than nice hair at this moment, however. She turned her collar up around the back of her neck and shoved her hands deeper into her pockets.

"Damn, it's cold. We'll be warm in a few minutes," Will said. "Wait right here."

She watched as he strode away in the lightly falling snow. She almost felt the first tingles of that same worry that had bothered her in the lobby but she pushed it to the back of her mind. She'd made her decision. She had two weeks of just being with Will before she had to deal with the fallout from it.

THE SLEIGH WAS big and looked like it had come from a scene from one of the Currier and Ives lithographs that had hung in her grandparents' hallway when she'd been little. The driver introduced himself to them and as Will talked to him, Penny moved to the front of the sleigh to get a closer look at the horses.

She'd grown up back East in a fairly suburban area, but her best friend growing up had been raised on a horse ranch and Penny had always loved the animals.

"Ready?" Will asked.

She nodded, even though she felt a little nervous. Hell, after the way her last relationship had broken down who would blame her…but she'd made her decision and it was time to enjoy it.

"This is for you," he said.

"I didn't get you anything," she responded, taking the long square box that was wrapped in plain brown paper and tied with a simple red bow.

"You can owe me," he said with a wink.

"Have you done this a hundred times before?"

"It's a little unflattering you think I'm old enough to have experienced a hundred Christmases," he said flippantly.

"You know what I meant." Penny held the package with one hand and just watched him, wondering if he'd been serious about not lying. She was sorely tempted to embark on a red-hot affair with this handsome stranger, but if he was going to hedge and evade questions, she'd call the whole thing off.

"I do. And to answer your question—no, this isn't my normal MO. But I have had two-week affairs before. As I mentioned earlier, I pretty much don't do long-term."

She nodded. "Should I open this gift now?"

"Yes. The driver has gone to get the hot cocoa I ordered."

Penny turned the box over in her hands. Her first present from Will. She untied the red ribbon and took a moment to slip it in her pocket. It was that soft fabric kind. Then she carefully undid the wrapping paper.

"I've never seen anyone take as long to open a present."

She laughed. "Sorry about that. I like to savor things."

He reached over, pulling off his glove, and touched the side of her face. His hand was warm against her skin. "Me, too."

She leaned over and kissed him, just a quick brushing of lips before removing the rest of the paper. He took it from her and wadded it up in his hand and tossed the ball of wrapping into the nearby trash bin. “Open it.”

She took the lid off the box and pushed the tissue paper aside to reveal a pretty, thick wool scarf. The colors were soft and muted, almost like the sky just after dawn. The wool was so soft that she couldn’t stop touching it. It was an exquisite gift. “Thank you.”

He nodded then reached into the box and took out the scarf. He stepped closer to her and wrapped it around her neck, tying it carefully before pulling her hair from the back where it had gotten trapped by the fabric.

“I really like it,” she said.

He cupped her face and tipped her head up so that their eyes met. Even in the darkness his were still brilliantly blue. “I really like you.”

He kissed her then, slowly, as if they had all the time in the world. Passion built inside her as his mouth moved over hers. His tongue was gentle but firm as he thrust it into her mouth and she dropped the box to the ground to reach for him. Putting her arms around his broad shoulders, pulling him close to her, she reveled in his power and strength. His chest was solid against hers even through the layers of their winter coats. And the snow that fell lightly around them was a counterpoint to the heat they generated.

He wrenched his lips from hers and then dropped a series of soft kisses on her face before he stepped back and bent to retrieve the box she’d dropped. He walked over to toss it in the trashcan. As he slowly headed back toward her, she watched the way he moved, with that confident stride and the languid grace of a man sure of himself and his woman. *His woman.* She had pretty much agreed to be that. Penny rubbed her lips, which still tingled from his kiss. She was electrified from his touch. Couldn't wait for him to kiss her again and to see how this evening turned out. What kind of lover would he be?

"Why are you watching me?"

"I like the way you move," she said, getting more excited by the prospect of this Christmas romance. There was no pressure to be what he wanted so they could make things work out. There was nothing for her to do except enjoy her time with him. Something about him just made her feel warm inside. When he was just a few feet away, she leaped toward him and saw a look of surprise before he opened his arms to catch her.

She laughed as he hugged her close and spun her around. She threw her head back as the snowflakes fell on her face and she released all the past hurts and emotional baggage that she normally carried with her. For this Christmas, she was ready to let go and enjoy it.

He slowly lowered her down the length of his body and she kissed him with all the fierce desire building up inside of her. She couldn't believe that it had only been this morning when she'd met him.

Savoring the moment, the feel of his lips ravaging hers, she marveled at how someone's world could change that quickly. How a chance encounter could completely make her open her eyes to a world she had never realized existed until now.

"I guess you like the scarf," he said wryly as he put her on her feet.

"I do. But I like you more. I think this is going to be the best Christmas I've had in a long time."

"Me, too," he murmured.

The attendant returned and the driver climbed into the front of the carriage while she and Will were seated in the back. The blankets they had for their legs were thick and woven in a traditional red, green and gold plaid. They were handed a thermos and two insulated mugs for their drinks, which were stowed in a small basket on the floor.

"Ready?" the driver asked.

They nodded and the sleigh took off, pulling them through the snow with only the sounds of their breathing, the bells on the horses' necks and the whistle of the blades over the snow to accompany them.

# 4

WILL WRAPPED HIS arm around Penny as the sleigh traveled over the path in the moonlight. The snow had stopped falling and the trees on either side of them were all aglow with white lights that made the snow twinkle as they moved past it. The high back of the sleigh kept them protected from the wind.

He hadn't expected his present to generate the reaction it had from her. She was cute and sexy and all signs pointed to her being everything he wanted in a lover. But he'd felt something else when she'd thanked him for the scarf.

A stirring of unfamiliar emotion that had been so intense he'd had to force it back down inside himself. He wanted Penny, he reiterated to himself. He was going to enjoy Christmas with a woman instead of by himself, but that was it.

"Do you know how to pick out any of the stars?" Penny asked, jarring him out of his thoughts. "I've always really liked looking up at them, but I'm afraid I can't ever pick any of the constellations out."

He tipped his head back, gazing up at the sky. "I know the basic ones. Like right there is the Little Dipper."

He pointed to it.

She looked up. "Do you see the star the wise men followed?"

"I can't really, but I bet we could find a bright star that would work."

"Or we could each find a star that is leading us," she said. "My mom used to do that whenever we couldn't find an answer. Or if we didn't have a tradition, she'd say let's make up something we both like."

He liked the sound of her mom. He'd come to terms with the fact that he'd never have that kind of family. His parents' death in a car crash had left him set for life financially, but there were times when he was reminded of the stuff he'd missed out on. Penny made him want to have that. She was spontaneous, he realized. The phone throwing, the jumping into his arms…

Did she always leap like that?

"Have you ever followed something like a star?" he asked curiously. It seemed like something she'd do. "Just took off believing it would lead you to something special?"

"No… Well, that's not true. One time I followed a dog I spotted after school. Every day after that, for a straight week, it waited for me outside of my classroom. I thought it was a stray and that maybe I could keep him."

She turned to face him, her pretty gaze serious, and she licked her pink lips. His eyes tracked the movement and his blood flowed thicker in his veins. "What happened next?"

"When I approached the dog it sort of took off, not running but just heading somewhere. I had saved half of my sandwich at lunch so I could sort of bribe the dog. It was a cute little poodle and in my head I'd named it Fifi."

"Sounds like you had a plan," he said.

"And a big imagination. It's part of the reason I'm good at creating events," she said. "So I followed Fifi and she turned down my street. I was eight at the time so please don't think this is too lame."

"I'd never think you were lame," he said, enjoying the way she told the story. Seeing how her eyes sparkled and hearing that note of excitement and joy in her voice was truly infectious.

"Okay, I was so excited. Fifi trotted past my house, but instead of stopping at my place, she ran straight past it. I followed her round the corner and saw her disappear through a redbrick house with a doggy door."

"I'm sorry you didn't get your dog," he said.

She laughed good-naturedly. "I was so disappointed, but it wasn't meant to be. I did have a fun adventure following the dog, though. And my mom got us a cute miniature dachshund when I told her the story." He thought about Penny's story. He'd never been that aware of his environment, sure he'd followed things on the internet, but in the real world he tended to just keep his head down and move forward. He couldn't remember ever being different even as a child.

"That's sweet."

"Thanks," she said. "She was good about making sure I had what I wanted. Not that I was spoiled or anything."

His lips twitched with humor. "Sure you weren't."

"It's hard to not be a little spoiled when you're the only child," she admitted with a cheeky grin.

"What about you? Spoiled? Siblings?" she asked.

"Only child, as well."

She arched her eyebrow at him. “We both are used to getting our way, then. That could make things interesting.”

“I wasn’t spoiled,” he said. He left it at that. He didn’t want to talk about his parents’ deaths or being raised by distant relatives. It created an image that he wasn’t comfortable sharing with her. They were temporary playmates, nothing more.

“Did you ever follow anything home?”

“No. I’m usually very focused on getting what I want. Instead of following dogs or stars, I’d use my computer and do a load of research before starting out.”

She rolled her eyes. “Sounds kind of boring.”

“Perhaps, but I don’t waste time and I get my end result every single time. I try to eliminate all the variables so I don’t have to deal with surprises.”

“But surprises are the best part of life,” she said.

“That hasn’t been my experience.”

Shaking her head at him, she countered, “That’s not true.”

He gave her a look from under his eyelashes.

She punched him playfully in the shoulder. “You’re wrong. Today I bet you weren’t expecting an iPhone to come flying through the air at you.”

She had him there. She knew it, too—he saw it on her face. “That’s true.”

“Also you didn’t expect that I’d be so intriguing,” she said.

*Right again.* He definitely hadn’t expected Penny, and he was learning that even though he’d thought he’d managed all the variables with this Christmas liaison, perhaps he had forgotten something very important. The Penny factor.

She was having fun—despite the fact that after the past few months, the stress of quitting her job and hoping for a new one, she still hadn't gotten the call she'd been hoping for today. But given that the East Coast was two hours ahead of them, she doubted they would be calling before tomorrow.

Her real life was still a mess but tonight that didn't seem to matter as much. Will had wrapped his arm around her shoulder and tucked her against his side. He had gone quiet after she'd told him about Fifi but maybe he was thinking…who knew what. The bells of the horses rang across the empty fields as they continued their ride, and she felt the hope and joy of the season all around her.

Suddenly, she found herself humming the beginning of "Jingle Bells" under her breath. The song was stuck in her head now. Ugh. She couldn't start singing. Wouldn't let herself do that.

But there it was.

"Dashing through the snow," Will said, under his breath, too.

She tipped her head back and started laughing. "Is that song also in your head?"

"It's impossible for it not to be. We are in the middle of a freakin' Norman Rockwell Christmas scene."

"I would have said Currier and Ives."

He shook his head. "You like to argue, don't you?"

She thought about that for a long minute. She did have to always make sure she had her own opinion. "I never thought of it that way. I just want to make sure I'm standing on my own, not following someone else."

"Me, too. And this is definitely Norman Rockwell. You'll never convince me otherwise."

"Are you sure?"

"How could you possibly? I've made my mind up and I never change it," he said.

"Never? Are you sure about that?"

He nodded. "I can promise you I will never change my mind. Once a decision has been made I stick to it."

"Duly noted," she said. It was something that she might see as a red flag if they were going to date long-term, but for two weeks…what did that matter? "Jingle bells, jingle bells…"

He squeezed her close, putting his finger under her chin, and when he tipped her head back, she looked up at the strong line of his jaw. There was a tiny birthmark under his chin. Something she wouldn't have noticed if they hadn't been sitting so close. She reached up and touched it.

"Beauty mark," she said.

"Beauty?"

"That's what my mom always calls them. She has one that looks like a strawberry along her neck, and she says it's a mark of inner beauty." Penny missed her mom but she was in the Caribbean with her new husband celebrating the holidays. Exhaling softly, she stroked his neck. It was strong and had the tiniest bit of beard stubble on it. His light brown hair brushed the side of his face and she pushed it out of the way.

"No one has ever suggested there was anything beautiful about me," he said gruffly.

She looked into those incredible blue eyes of his and wondered about this man. She had a bunch of questions about his past. What had shaped him into the person he was today? Why would anyone be satisfied with two-week relationships?

But she kept those questions to herself. "You have to know you are a very beautiful man."

"Rugged maybe. And I get charming a lot…but beauty? Nah." She understood where he was coming from. But there was something about his confidence and the way he pushed her to take him on his terms that contributed to what she saw when she looked at him.

Or at least what she saw now, on this magical snow ride. "Well, we can agree to disagree."

"Which we've already established you like to do," he said, winking at her.

She pretended to elbow him in the gut. Playing around to control her emotions so she didn't let things turn too serious. "Keep it up and I'll show you what a fierce competitor I can be."

"Are you one?"

She shrugged. "I sometimes say it doesn't really matter to me if I win, but it does. I hate losing. Not that I want to beat anyone else—I just like being right."

She laughed and so did he.

"Me, too." He rubbed his chin on the top of her head and held her lightly in his arms.

"What are you thinking?" she whispered.

Their sleigh ride was getting close to its end and the snow started to fall a little more heavily. They huddled together but the snow was cold as it fell on them. Will maneuvered around and pulled the blanket up over their backs and then their heads. She looked at him and realized how safe he'd made her feel tonight.

Not just physically safe, but emotionally. He'd listened to her and didn't judge her. Just let her be who she was. Probably because they weren't trying to impress each other. Though, frankly, he'd more than done that with dinner, the gift and this sleigh ride. She had relaxed her guard.

He kissed the tip of her nose as they returned to the Lodge. "Thank you for making this a very special night."

She shook her head in bewilderment. "How have I done that?"

"By sharing your stories and that sparkle that I think might just be you."

"I *sparkle*?" she asked with a giggle. "Did you really just say that?"

He freed them both from the blanket and stood up, holding his hand out to her. She took it and he helped her to her feet and then out of the sleigh.

She stood to one side as he thanked the driver and tipped him and then turned back to her. The snow still fell over him, making him look even more strikingly handsome, and for a moment she wondered if she might have made a huge mistake. This arrangement was just supposed to be about having fun, but she saw signs that Will might be the kind of man she wanted in her life for a lot longer than one Christmas.

TWO DAYS LATER, Will walked through the quaint Park City streets looking for some new ski gear. He and Penny had said good-night at her front door after their sleigh ride and he'd walked away without a kiss. But the ride hadn't gone exactly to plan. He had meant it as a prelude to seduction but the truth was he liked her. She stirred things deep inside him that he liked to pretend he never felt and didn't care about.

But that was a lie.

He'd always been one of those men who knew where he was going. When he'd gotten out of rehab, he'd made choices that had pointed him toward his future. He eliminated all the things that were enablers for him.

First order of business: he'd stopped partying 24/7 and started working. A part of him found it surprising that he had the golden touch when it came to making money. But he had found his niche and that was enough for him. However, two nights ago, he'd felt like that had begun to change. He hadn't slept well since then and he wondered if he would again.

And it was all *her* fault.

As Will continued his stroll through the town, he paused at the corner where a mural of the Wasatch Mountain Range was on the side of Fresh Sno's retail store. It was really well done.

"Nice picture, eh?"

He glanced over his shoulder to see Penny standing there. She had a Fresh Sno bag in one hand. Her blond hair was hanging around her shoulders under a pink knit hat. Her coat was a deep turquoise wool and she had it buttoned to the top with the scarf he'd given her wrapped around her neck.

"Yes, it is. Are you following me?" he asked with a grin. For the first time in a long time, he was struggling to keep his flirtations light. He knew that was a danger sign. It might be better for both of them if he just walked away now. They hadn't even slept together. No harm, no foul.

"Following you? No, not at all. I decided I need a little retail therapy and my friend Bradley owns this place. He's the guy half of my cutesy friend couple. I stopped by to get some new ski gear. Want to join me on the slopes?"

Just like that, she made it seem normal that he hadn't

talked to her in one entire day. They had only a limited number of days to spend together and he'd wasted one.

"Sorry about not being able to see you yesterday." He'd sent her a note via the hotel concierge desk that he'd had to work.

"It's fine. To be honest, this arrangement is harder for me than I thought it would be. But I understand about having work commitments so it's not a big deal." She spared him a look. "Of course, if we were a *real* couple, it might have bothered me. But that's clearly not the case..."

Work had been a convenient excuse, but he'd needed distance and now he regretted it. He'd never been a coward— *Ha!* his conscience jibed. Alcohol had been his crutch a long time ago and now it seemed like Penny was.

"Any word from the people in New York on your new job?" he asked.

"Just that they were still weighing their options and would be getting back to me in the new year. So I have nothing else to do in the meantime." She flashed him a coy look. "And the way I see it, I have two options here. I can either distract myself by having fun with you, *or* I can just relive my interview over and over again, trying to come up with all the things I could have done better."

He was willing to bet she'd wowed them. Penny had that thing that made people notice her. Made her stand out.

"I don't want to be responsible for all that misery," he deadpanned. "So skiing? That's your idea for today?"

"Yes. I'm not an expert at it, and I'm certainly not very daring, but I do like to spend a few hours on the slopes. Want to join me?"

"I would enjoy that. But I could use some new ski gear, too," he said. "That's why I'm here at Fresh Sno. I've heard about the brand and directed several of my investment clients toward them, so I thought I'd check out their retail space."

"I'll leave you to your shopping, then. Want to meet me at the ski rental at the Lodge in two hours?" She was being more cautious with him today. But then in the light of day that wasn't too surprising. Night seemed to be the time for daring.

"Want to join me? Where else are you going?"

"That kitchen shop up the block. I need some sprinkles for cookies," she said.

"I think the ones at the Lodge's bakery come with sprinkles."

She flashed a grin. "They do, wise guy, but I'm making my own. I mean you have to bake cookies at Christmas. I think it's a law or something."

"I've never done it. I hope the cops don't find out," he said.

"You're kidding, right?"

He shook his head.

"That's sad, Will. *Really* sad. You've spent your whole life missing out on eating the batter and broken cookies."

He wrinkled his nose. "I'm not sure that's a bad thing."

She nodded. "Well, it is. I'm not baking cookies until Saturday. Want to come to my place and help me?"

"Okay," he said. "I'll do that. Which kitchen store are you going to?"

She pointed to the big chain kitchen store down the block. The streets were draped with festive garland. "If you meet me there after you get your ski gear, you can pick out a couple of cookie cutters, too."

He nodded. "Sounds like a plan."

She smiled at him. "Later then."

He stood where he was, watching her walk away and wondering when he'd lost control of this affair. He had a feeling that it had started the moment her cell phone had come flying out of nowhere. As soon as he'd seen that pink jewel-covered case, and those long legs, he should have run in the opposite direction.

She was different than what he was used to. He didn't know if that would have any impact on him, but he hoped not. He didn't want his world to change.

Change. It was the one thing he feared the most. But he was coming to realize that there was a certain thrill in facing his fears, and he certainly wasn't ready to throw in the towel where Penny was concerned.

# 5

THE KITCHEN STORE was jam-packed with high-end appliances and prepackaged baking mixes. But what Penny was interested in wasn't the baking section. Why hadn't Will ever baked Christmas cookies? She didn't mean as a man, but as a kid. Even her co-workers all had stories, men and women alike, of being in the kitchen at the holidays. Even if they didn't bake them, most men stood in the kitchen, pretended to decorate and ate them fresh out of the oven.

It was one of those things she and her mom had made a tradition of when Penny was about ten. Prior to that, they'd bought cookies from a small mom-and-pop place that was a few blocks from their house. But the bakery had closed since the couple wanted to retire and move to Florida, so her mother had suggested they make their own. Penny had a chuckle at the way they'd both been very unskilled at first, but over the years, they had gotten a lot better. Still smiling to herself, she browsed the baking section. Her chalet had a small kitchen with a tiny oven so she took a few moments to get all the necessities.

"Is an elf going to be cooking with you?" Will said

as he joined her like they'd agreed. He reached into her basket to remove the small spatula she'd just tossed in her bag.

"No, silly. That's a cookie spatula—it enables you to get the cookies from the tray without scrunching them up."

He furrowed his dark brow. "Interesting. What kind of cookies are you making?"

"We are making a basic sugar-cookie dough and then rolling it out, cutting it into cookies, baking them and then frosting them."

"Sounds like a lot of work," he said with a grimace. "I think I might have to wait for the *eating them* part. Maybe just supervise you working..."

"Are you good at supervising?"

"If I'm honest?"

Penny nodded but was only half listening to his answer. She bit her lower lip as she looked at him, with his thick brown hair falling loosely around his face and scarf tied nonchalantly around his neck. Part of her wished she'd just invited him back to her chalet two nights ago. Got rid of the desire that made it impossible for her to do anything but watch his lips move and wonder how they'd feel on her skin.

She wanted him. She'd dreamed of him in her bed last night. And she knew that today, unless he really screwed up, somehow she was going to have him there. Two days were gone of her fourteen with him. She didn't want to waste another second like she had yesterday by giving him space to work. She was in as much control of this affair as he was.

"What?" she asked, upon realizing he'd stopped talking and was staring at her.

"I said I'm not good at supervising but I can tell you are. Are you okay?"

She tipped her head to the side. "I'm…fine. I was just, uh, looking at your hair and wondering how it would feel between my fingers. I really didn't get to touch it when we were on our sleigh ride because I had my gloves on."

His eyes darkened and he stepped closer to her in the busy shop. No one was paying them the least bit of attention, as they were all busy getting their own purchases made. He stood pressed against her front, the cookie-cutter baskets to her back, and he put his hands lightly on her waist, bringing his face so close to her that each exhalation of his breath brushed over her mouth.

His breath was minty again, his aftershave outdoorsy, and she breathed it all in. Breathed *him* in. Closed her eyes and tried to make a sense memory that she could carry with her forever. But then she forced her eyes open. Not forever. Just for Christmas.

"Touch it now," he said.

She lifted her hand and tangled her fingers in the thick, rich strands of his dark hair. It was cool from him being outdoors without a hat on and a few snowflakes that hadn't melted were caught in it. She pulled her fingers downward, letting the strands spread out and then fall back against his head.

He had his eyes half-closed and watched her carefully. She felt her pulse racing and her blood seemed to be pumping a lot faster. She wanted him.

Penny licked her lips, which felt dry, and noticed he tracked the movement with his half-hooded gaze. She felt his hands in her hair, slowly winding a lock around his finger before letting it go. They he cupped the back of her head, spread his fingers out and angled her head before he brought his mouth down on hers.

The kiss was quick and hot. Full of passion and promise, determination and desire. He wanted her, too.

He pulled back and her lips were tingling and every nerve in her body awakened. Suddenly skiing and baking cookies didn't seem like anything she had to do today. She wanted to find a private place and rip his clothes off. Explore the rest of his body and then take him and make him hers.

Someone bumped into them and Penny looked down into the face of a five-year-old girl with a gap-toothed grin.

"I'm looking for a princess cookie cutter," she said. "Can you help me?"

Will laughed and stepped back, crouching next to the little girl to start searching in the baskets with her. And Penny took several breaths to try to feel normal again, but as she picked through the cookie cutters, she had a sinking feeling that she wasn't going to find her way back to normal that easily.

She found a tiara and finally a princess cutter. "Here you go."

"Thank you," the little girl said, racing away.

Will had two in his hands when he stood up.

"What do you have there?"

"A rolling pin-shaped cookie cutter, because I never want to forget standing in this store with you," he said with a devilish gleam in his eye, "and a sleigh."

She took his cutters and added them to her basket. The cashier was friendly as they approached, smiling warmly at them.

"You are the cutest couple," she gushed.

Penny realized she didn't know how to respond, but Will threw his arm over her shoulder. "Yes, we are."

THEY TOOK TWO runs down the slopes before calling it a day. For Will, if he'd been on his own, he would have kept skiing, but honestly even the most interesting ski slopes couldn't compare to the excitement he felt with Penny.

He'd been turned on since the cookware shop, and their ride back to the Lodge and then up the mountain on the ski lift hadn't changed that. The bulk of their afternoon had been touching, sort of kissing and a lot of teasing.

He thought that Penny knew she was keeping him in a state of semiarousal with those teasing touches, and it really didn't bother him too much since he had plans to end all the teasing tonight.

"Want to warm up by the fire pit?" he asked after they'd turned their skis back in to the rental stand.

"I'd love to. Grab our spot and I'll get us a couple of hot drinks," she said.

"That's nice, but I'm the white knight, remember? Why don't you sit down and I'll get the drinks?"

She gave him a sweet smile. "That's very old-fashioned. But I like it."

"Cocoa?"

"Sounds great," she said.

He watched as Penny took a seat and went to the bar to order their drinks. She glanced up and caught him watching so he pulled out his phone to check his email instead. He needed to keep his priorities straight. There wasn't anything urgent on his phone, and he shoved it into his pocket trying to pretend that he didn't feel tense again.

"Hello," the bartender said. "What can I get you to drink?"

"Cocoa please. Two of them."

"Enjoying a getaway with the girlfriend?" the bartender asked as he made the drinks.

"Um…yes, I am." But Penny wasn't his girlfriend. Not the way the bartender meant it.

Normally when he went away for Christmas it wasn't this Christmassy. He went to the Caribbean and stayed at all-inclusive resorts and just hung out on the beach or in his beachfront room with his lover.

There were no holiday-themed dates in the Caribbean. So different from this year. The very essence of what he was doing with Penny was holiday-themed.

A part of him was okay with that because each year needed to be different. Snow instead of sand this year. He had no desire to be like Bill Murray in the movie *Groundhog Day*, reliving his life over and over again.

He hoped he'd learned and moved on.

But as he watched her walking toward him, he realized he was skating on a very fine edge. He had to be careful to remember that no matter how much this seemed like a "real" holiday, it was still a two-week dalliance. And that was it.

That was all it could be. She was smiling as she sauntered toward him, and he had that feeling that he was on the cusp of something that could change him. Maybe he should just walk away now. Because if he were completely honest with himself, he'd have to admit that sex might not be enough with her. That even an afternoon of skiing left him wanting to do a lot more with her.

He handed her a mug of frothy hot cocoa before sitting down next to her.

"Do you like whipped cream?" she asked.

"I do," he said. Then realized that even if he didn't, he might be tempted to drink it just to see her keep on smiling. There was something about her smile that got to him.

"You are a really good skier," she remarked.

"Thank you. When I was young, when my parents were still alive, we used to ski every winter. I grew up on the slopes."

"You can tell. So your parents are dead?" she asked, then made a face. "I know that sounds dumb and wasn't a very tactful way of saying it. I'm sorry about your mom and dad."

"It's okay," he said. "They died when I was ten. I was already signed up for boarding school and summer camps so my relatives who inherited my care weren't burdened by me."

"*Burdened* by you?" she asked incredulously. "That's not a very nice way of saying that. Didn't they want you?"

How had he gotten on this topic? He was usually more careful with how he talked about his past. "All I meant is they had busy lives and I was already established in mine."

She wrinkled her nose at him. "I'm not sure if I should hug you because of that, but you seem okay with it. Was there any fallout to growing up that way?"

He definitely wasn't going to get into all that. "One perk is that I get to spend my holidays in the company of lovely women like you."

She pursed her lips. "That's…flippant. But I guess that's all that we really have between us."

He shook his head. "It isn't. Already you feel different to me, but we both know we are going back to our real worlds on January 1."

The reminder wasn't just for Penny; it was also for himself. He'd tried relationships in the past, and if he was being honest, they simply didn't work for him. He'd shut down all of his emotions when his parents died. He'd been left alone and hadn't really understood how to cope. There were no relatives clamoring to take him in and he'd been sent back to school and camp. Not having a "home" after his parents died had left something broken inside of him. He knew that.

"Don't worry. I'm not looking for serious," she promised him. "Just fun. Christmas fun! With a man who could ski me under the table, but stuck to the moderate runs. Thank you for doing that."

"Why would I want to ski by myself when I could share it with you?" he said huskily.

She smiled at him. "I will say this—whoever taught you to talk to women did a very good job."

"How so?"

"You seem to always know the right thing to say," she said.

He winked. "I like to think it's part of my charm."

"It might be," she said.

They sipped their cocoa and talked about current events, but he noticed she'd stopped the teasing touches and worried that she might have changed her mind about a no-strings-attached affair.

IT WAS REASSURING to hear Will's comments. Really, it was. That's what Penny told herself as she stood in the living area of her chalet and painted her toenails before she went to see Will later that evening.

He wasn't going to change the rules halfway through this. He'd said two weeks, he meant two weeks. That was what she'd wanted to hear. What she'd needed to hear. He said he wouldn't lie to her and he hadn't.

Except now she sort of wished he had. She sort of needed him to at least pretend—what? That he'd changed his mind? Well, she wasn't going to change hers. She wasn't ready for a serious relationship. Not now.

She had to sort out her real life and figure out her next steps—she had no time for a man. Even one who made her remember all the reasons why she wanted a lover in her life.

The day had turned unexpectedly for her when she'd seen Will in town. She'd enjoyed flirting with him all afternoon, and touching him had been pure bliss. God, she wanted him. She knew that the sex probably wouldn't be as good as she was anticipating. Nothing against Will… it was simply that in the past, when she'd had this much buildup, the guy came after three thrusts and she was left lying there wondering what the heck had happened.

But another part of her was convinced he might be the best lover she'd ever have. So far he was an ace at shattering all of her illusions. Every time she thought she had him figured out, he did something else to force her to look at him again.

For instance, this afternoon when he'd talked about losing his parents so nonchalantly, it had been like a knife in her heart. No child should think of themselves that way—of "not being a burden" to the adults in their life. But Will did. He hadn't said it to gain her sympathy or anything like that, just stated a fact that would warp a lesser man.

To be fair, there was something maybe a little damaged about only wanting a two-week relationship, but he seemed to be okay with it.

Now she just had to be okay with it, too.

She finished painting her nails and leaned back on the couch, putting her feet on the coffee table. With a heavy sigh, she stared up at the ceiling. What was wrong with her? She owed it to Will to keep her emotions in check.

Her mind was still going a million miles a minute when her phone rang. She glanced at the screen to see Elizabeth's name on the caller ID.

She contemplated not answering it, but Elizabeth was her best friend. The one she could talk to about anything. "Hey," she said before she changed her mind and chickened out.

"Hey, you. I'm calling to see if you'd like to have dinner with me tonight. Bradley is heading to Europe for a few days on business."

"I can't tonight," she said. "Maybe tomorrow?"

"Okay, sounds good. What are you doing tonight?" Elizabeth asked. "It's none of my business but I'm nosey."

Penny laughed. "Remember that hottie I almost hit with my phone? I might see him later."

"Sounds like fun," Elizabeth said.

"I'm sure it will be," Penny replied. She just had to remember that it was the holidays. She could be free and do what she wanted to do. There were no rules that said every guy she dated had to have the potential to be the one. Hell, half the time she never thought beyond the next date, but because she and Will had set a time frame, all she could hear was the clock ticking down the days until he was gone.

"Are you okay?" Elizabeth asked.

"Yes, I'm fine. Will is a lot of fun. We went skiing

this afternoon and I'm sure he has some over-the-top romantic thing planned for tonight."

It was just like Will to do that. She didn't know much about him, if she was being honest, but she had realized that romance was something he was good at. And she supposed if a man asked a woman to have a short-term affair it was in his best interest to make it the best two weeks of her romantic life.

"Like what? I'm not very good at romantic gestures. Maybe I can steal a few ideas and blow Bradley's socks off."

"He took me on a sleigh ride on our first date. It was sweet and sexy."

"Have you slept with him?"

"Elizabeth!"

Her friend didn't say anything for a few minutes. "Did you?"

"Not yet. I want to. But he's so good at being all the things I want in a man, and you know my past with lovers hasn't been great…so I'm sort of afraid to. I don't want it to ruin that perfect image I have of him."

"Fair enough, but if he's as good at romance and all the other stuff as you say, I'm willing to bet he won't let you down in bed."

That was what she was afraid of. If he were a disappointing lover it would be a lot easier to accept that this would end.

"I've got to go, hon," Elizabeth said a moment later. "Bradley is calling me on the other line. But I want to hear all about this hot date tomorrow."

"Of course," Penny said, hoping she'd have something

good to tell her friend. She knew she just had to get her head around this Christmas present she was giving herself. But it was a lot harder than she'd anticipated.

# 6

WILL HAD PLANNED the evening carefully. He was tired of waiting and suspected Penny was, too. Tonight that would end.

He'd take her to his bed, make love to her, and she'd go back to being like every other woman he'd ever met. Although he was happy with his plan, it had to go off without a hitch. Which meant that the ambiance had to be ultraromantic. To that end, he'd ordered dinner from the Lodge's Cajun-inspired restaurant, and had the food warming in the little kitchenette. He had a blanket spread out on the floor, and had even asked the staff at the Lodge to decorate the mantle with garland and brightly colored Christmas lights. Glancing around the room, he smiled to himself. It had taken some finesse, but finally everything was the exact way he wanted it to be. After smoothing his hands over the blanket one last time to make sure it was soft enough for Penny, he checked the timers on the oven and the bottle of red wine he had opened, then got his coat on and left to go and collect his date.

He adjusted the wreath on the front of his door and

flicked on the switch to the lights, which framed his entryway. Now the exterior of his place looked just as festive as the inside, and as he stepped out into the lightly falling snow, he let the wind and the snowflakes carry away his apprehension about pursuing a relationship with Penny.

Somehow he'd managed to mess himself up when it came to this woman by letting her grow too big in his imagination. Once they had sex, however, and this settled down to something similar to his normal dating routine, everything would be fine.

He arrived at her chalet and knocked on her door.

"Coming."

He waited, looking distractedly at the tiny Santas that were dotted around the wreath on her front door.

"Hello," she said as she opened it.

A wave of warm air surrounded him and he caught his breath as Penny stood there in a form-fitting black velvet dress that ended at her midthigh. She had her blond hair curled and then piled high on her head with a tendril on either side framing her face.

Her blue eyes sparkled and her lipstick was shiny, drawing his eyes to her mouth. He leaned in for a kiss before he could think better of it. She pulled back.

"No mistletoe."

"I didn't think I needed mistletoe to kiss you," he murmured.

"That depends," she said coyly.

"On?"

"If you will give me time to fix my lipstick before we leave," she replied, with a tinkling laugh that made his gut clench and his cock harden. He wanted her. He realized he'd been carefully playing a game with himself and not with her. He had been trying so hard to make her blend into the pack of women he'd had in his life when she clearly stood out.

"You won't need to. We are having dinner at my place," he said.

She reached for a long cream-colored wool coat and handed it to him. "So I guess we're done with playing the slow game?"

"I am," he said, looking her in the eye. "Aren't you?"

She nodded. "But to be honest, I'm kind of nervous. I keep making myself more and more anxious by trying to make this—"

"Don't overthink it, sweetheart. It's just you and me. There are no right or wrong actions here. Just whatever feels right to us." He smiled down at her. "And if we just enjoy dinner by my fireplace and you want to go home alone, then that is what will happen."

She smiled back. "Thank you."

"You're welcome," he said, taking her coat and holding it up for her to put on.

Despite his outward bravado, Will realized her nerves mirrored his own. There was something different about her…and maybe it was just that he was experiencing a white Christmas, or the fact that it had been two years since he'd had a holiday affair, but something made Penny seem special.

The Penny factor.

He kept forgetting that. As soon as she had her coat on, she closed and locked her door and looked over at him. She licked her lips and tipped her head to the side as she watched him.

He let his gaze drift down over her from the top of her head to those ridiculously sexy high-heeled stilettos she wore on her feet. She was pure temptation and he didn't have to deny himself. It was a heady feeling. Made him feel like he was on a wild binge and on the edge of doing something crazy. Much the same as he had back in the days when he used to drink too much.

He lifted her off her feet and swung her up in his arms. She clutched his shoulders and asked breathlessly, "What are you doing?"

"You're wearing heels. Not ideal for walking on a snowy path," he said, walking carefully down the steps toward said path.

"No one has ever carried me before. I mean my mom probably did when I was little, but I can't remember anyone carrying me."

"I'm glad," he replied. He wondered where her father was. She never mentioned the man, but that was *real life.* Not this special, magical Christmas they had promised to spend together.

"I like it," she said giddily. "I might let you carry me again."

He planned to carry her to his bed later tonight, but for right now he was content to set her on her feet at the front door of his chalet. He unlocked it and held the door open for her.

Will took her coat and hung it on the peg near the door, and then pulled her into his arms for the kiss that she'd denied him earlier. She came up on her tiptoes, meeting him halfway, and put her hands firmly on his shoulders. Her lips parted under his as he thrust his tongue deep into her mouth.

She moaned and leaned forward, brushing her breasts against his chest. He slipped his hands down to her waist, lifted her off her feet again, and spun so that he was leaning against the wall and could hold her nestled against him.

Penny's hands slid up his shoulders to his neck. Her fingers stroked his neck and his erection grew with each touch. She sucked his lower lip between her teeth and bit down carefully, then pulled back.

"Dinner first," she said.

Nodding, he set her down and away from him. He gestured for her to go into the living room as he went to the kitchen area. "Would you like a glass of wine?"

"Yes, please," she said.

He poured her one and then poured himself a highball glass of Perrier. "To new beginnings."

She lifted her glass to his and took a sip. "You don't drink?"

"No, I don't."

She perched on one of the stools that were set by the breakfast bar, putting her wineglass on the counter. "Why not?"

"I used to drink too much. Found I was losing control and decided I didn't like it. So I stopped."

She narrowed her eyes at him. "Why is it that everything that happens to you fits into some neat explanation?"

"How do you mean?" he asked, setting his glass next to hers on the counter and taking out the tray of cheese, bread and olives he'd prepared for an appetizer.

"Just that you seem to bottle everything up in a neat little jar after you deal with it."

He led the way to the living room and heard her following. "Can you sit in that skirt?"

She nodded. "But I'm not going to unless you give me some answers."

"I promise you I will," he said, offering her his hand as he set the tray on the blanket. She walked over, carefully sitting down, and a moment later he joined her.

He didn't like to talk about his problems. Drinking, lack of parents, the fact that he sometimes had to deal with some unexplained anger. He'd managed all of these things by carefully putting them in compartments and locking them away.

"I'm waiting," she said carefully. "I've known a few friends who have had addiction problems, and not one of them could have an open bottle of wine in their home and not drink it."

He leaned back against the sofa and took a moment to figure out the best way to answer her. The truth of course had to be an element of his answer, but *his* version of it. He didn't want her to see him too clearly.

"Tonight there is little chance that I will be in the state of mind where I'd be tempted to drink. I knew I was having you over, and with you, I'm focused entirely on the night to come."

She took a sip of her wine and then set her glass down. "So if you were alone you wouldn't have wine here?"

"No, I wouldn't. I know what my triggers are and a date with a pretty women isn't one of them," he said, reaching for a piece of baguette and spreading some of the soft herbed cheese on it. He held it out to her.

She took it but didn't seem interested in eating. "This is difficult. I know we said this is just temporary, but I want to know you. It's odd because already there are things about myself that I've shared with you that normally I wouldn't."

"Like what?" He wanted to know so he could understand her better. Figure out what it was that made her tick…what made her different.

"The story about following Fifi. Kissing in the cooking store. Okay…that wasn't something I said, but something I did. I'm not a PDA kind of girl. This feels too big."

"It's not any bigger than you and I. And just for the record, Penny, I don't kiss women in public. The way I am with you is special." He scrubbed a hand across his face. "Most of the time I don't like to talk about myself. There is something about dredging up my past that makes… Well, I don't like to go there."

"Then why have you?" she prodded gently.

"Because you asked me for the truth. I said I would give it to you and I am a man of my word," he said.

"Okay. Well, I'm glad to hear that," she said. "I'm sorry about your addiction, and to be honest, I'm okay with not having wine. So from now on, why don't we just skip the alcohol?"

"It's not going to tempt me," he reiterated. "I've been sober for a long time."

"Oh, okay," she said. But he could tell that it wasn't.

"What is it? Why is this a hot button for you?"

She shrugged.

"The truth street goes two ways," he reminded her.

She chewed her lower lip and then looked away from him. "My dad was an addict. That's why he wasn't around when I was growing up and isn't a part of my life now. He just never could handle it."

Will leaned over, shifting so that they were eye to eye and she'd be able to read the truth in his gaze. "If I'd had people in my life who'd cared for me, I'd never have started drinking. And it's the fact that I don't want to lose anyone I love again that has kept me from committing to a long-term relationship."

She swallowed. "So two weeks is really all we're going to have?"

"Yes. I told you I'm a man of my word."

She nodded. "Okay, I believe you. Let's enjoy this dinner. I didn't mean to bring you down."

"You didn't. We needed to share these things. And to be honest, I was curious about your dad." He reached over and stroked her cheek. "Like you said, we aren't just lovers. I want us to be friends even after we part ways on New Year's Eve."

"I'd like that, too," she said softly. The timer went off in the kitchen and he got up to take care of the dinner. He turned it off and leaned back against the counter, unsure of how to move forward. Each thing he learned about Penny made it harder and harder to keep his promise to himself. To reassure himself that she was just like every other woman.

PENNY NEVER THOUGHT of her dad and she wasn't about to let thoughts of him ruin her night with Will. She put her wine to the side then stood up and walked around his little chalet. It was the mirror of hers and she noticed that he'd had some decorations for the holidays put up. Or maybe he'd put them up himself.

She wandered around the room as Will was in the kitchen area working. She felt odd. Not really herself. This truth thing wasn't as great as she'd thought it would be. And a part of her realized that was because not all lies that were told between couples were like the horrible one Butch had been living. Most of the time they were told to protect one other.

"Want to put some music on?" he asked.

"Yes," she said, picking up her wineglass and setting it on the counter next to the Bose speaker system. "Then I'll help you with dinner."

"No need. I've got it under control," he told her.

She took her iPhone and put it in the dock, then flipped through her playlists, looking for something that would be good for dinner. Lana Del Rey and "Summertime Sadness" didn't seem right. She settled on a playlist she used when she was working on planning events. A mix of adult contemporary songs mixed with some top-forty hits.

Then she leaned her elbows on the counter and watched as Will worked. She was back in that place where things were starting to get gray again. She wanted to fix that problem he had with shoving everything into his safely labeled jars. That wasn't healthy. Something she knew from personal experience.

"Why are you staring at me?"

"Just admiring your butt. I don't think I noticed how cute it was before," she said lightly. Enough truth had been shared for tonight. Time to remember she was young and this was a temporary affair.

He turned his back to her and looked over his shoulder with a wink. "Like the view?"

"Very much. What do you do to stay in shape? I can tell you like to ski and I did notice you have sun lines on your face."

"Pretty much anything I can. I love being outside. I work long hours on my computer, but I always take the weekends for myself. I compete or train for a lot of cycling road races. What about you?"

"Nothing that ambitious. I'm doing that run for breast

cancer with my friends in May so I've been training, but it's kind of hit-or-miss. I don't mind running once I get dressed and get outside, but convincing myself to get out of bed when the alarm goes off is hard."

"You lack motivation," he said.

"I do," she said with a grin. "So what's for dinner?"

"Cajun-inspired salmon and dirty rice."

"Sounds delicious," she said.

"I thought so," he replied with a wink. He carried their plates to the blanket and she brought the bread basket and the cutlery. As they dined it was easy to fall back into the rapport that had been between them from the beginning. She ate and listened to his tales from college Mardi Gras trips he'd taken when he'd been young and, as he put it, a little too wild.

"Spring Break was never my thing. And Mardi Gras sounds like it would be so packed and just too many people acting nuts for me."

"Like your crazy people in smaller doses?" he countered.

"Or not at all. I like crowds when I'm controlling an event so I at least have the illusion that I am in control. That I'm taking care of everything and staying one step ahead."

"That's part of my job at times. Analyzing risks and then mitigating them."

"Does it work?" she asked. "In business it's easier to predict, don't you think?"

He took her plate and carried it into the kitchen before he came back and sat closer to her. He pulled her into his arms so that she was nestled against his chest and they were both facing the roaring fire.

"I think business is sort of easier to predict. Markets

have trends and you can spot them. But sometimes I am wrong and then I have a huge loss."

She snuggled against him. "What do you do then?"

"Regroup, figure out what I read wrong and make sure I don't do it again," he said.

"Wow, you must be pretty good to never make the same mistake twice," she mused.

"Not really. I try not to but sometimes I'm tempted to go down a path just because it seems like it might be worth the risk," he said, tipping her head back and looking down into her eyes.

There was some emotion in his eyes that she couldn't read. She wanted to ask him another question but he leaned down and kissed her. Not like their previous ones, but this was sweet and leisurely. An awakening of the passion that had been simmering between them since the moment they'd met. She knew that all the talk of being hurt had been masking her very real fear that she'd made the wrong choice when she'd agreed to be with Will.

But his mouth on hers and his tongue slowly seducing her with those long, languid movements made her push those doubts aside. She knew there was no place she'd rather be on this cold December night than right here in Will's arms.

# 7

PENNY SHIFTED AROUND until she was kneeling next to Will, and then straddled his lap, something her short skirt accommodated very easily. She framed his face with her hands, relishing the feel of his strong jaw under her fingers.

"Thank you for a very nice dinner."

"I like the way you say thank you," he said in response.

She kissed him again. His lips were soft yet firm under hers. She pushed herself up on her knees so that he slanted his head back against the cushions of the couch. She felt his hands on her hips, sliding up and down the sides of her thighs and then cupping her butt and squeezing.

She tilted her head for deeper access to his mouth. Thrust her tongue in again and again. God, his taste was addicting, but she shoved that thought out of her mind.

She pulled her mouth from his and dropped soft kisses along the line of his jaw to his ear. She settled back down on his lap, felt the firm ridge of his erection between her legs and rocked against it. He was so long and thick between her legs.

She shivered a little as a pulse of desire went through her entire body. Her breasts felt fuller in the cups of her bra and her nipples started to harden.

He groaned and squeezed her butt as his hips jerked forward to rub against her. She sat back on her heels, felt the buckle on her ankle strap sting her foot, but she didn't want to stop touching Will long enough to remove them.

She had a plan to do a striptease for him when the time was right. She'd read a lot of articles over the years, trying to make her love life more exciting, and finally she had a guy who might be the right one to test it out on.

She slowly unbuttoned his shirt, pausing to kiss each bit of his chest that was revealed. He had a light covering of hair on his chest that tapered from his pectorals down to his belly button. She scooted back and untucked the tails of his shirt from his pants and then spread it open so she could look her fill at his taut chest.

He flexed his muscles as she looked at him. "Like what you see?"

"I do," she admitted. Penny ran her finger down the center of his body from his Adam's apple, following the line of his sternum. Then she leaned in, inhaling the scent of his aftershave combined with his own natural musk. She lowered her mouth and dropped nibbling kisses on his neck, then shifted to caress her way down his chest. A few exquisite moments later, she bit at the flat flesh around his belly button and then leaned back to see his reaction.

He had his arms spread on the cushions behind him and his head was tipped back again. She leaned up to take his mouth again in a slow, tantalizing kiss that left no doubt how much she wanted him.

She thrust her tongue deep and tangled it with his as she shifted on his lap, rocking her center over the ridge of his cock. Breathing hard, she scraped one fingernail over his chest, found his flat nipples and teased them, then let her touch roam lower.

Penny pulled her mouth from his and he ran his fingers through her hair, bringing her mouth back down to his. She shifted a little, let him dominate the kiss for a few moments, forgetting that she was seducing him, exploring him.

Making Will hers. Unwrapping him like he was the one Christmas present she'd been waiting a lifetime to find. She didn't want to think, just feel. Just make this as physical as it could be. She felt his hand on the back of her thigh and wished she hadn't worn sheer tights under her dress.

Pulling her mouth from his, she leaned forward to start kissing her way down his body again. This time she shifted even farther back so she could get to his flat stomach. She reached for his belt and slowly undid it.

Once she drew it through the loops, she tossed it aside. He shifted his hips forward, rubbing his cock against her hand. She curved her fingers around his length and tightened her grip as he shafted her hand.

She unfastened his pants, pushing her hand inside to fondle him through his boxers, stroking up and down while she shifted again so she could kiss him. But just briefly. She skimmed her tongue over his jaw before she leaned in to whisper in his ear. "Are you ready for me?"

She felt him shiver in response, and when his cock jerked under her hand, she claimed his lips once more.

"Hell, Penny, I'm more than ready for you," he bit out, his voice raw and husky as he drew his hand down the center of her back.

She felt like she was already on the edge of her climax and she wasn't ready for it yet. Wanted to draw this moment out for as long as she could.

"Good," she said, pushing herself off his lap and standing up. She spread her legs as she drew the skirt of her dress up toward her waist, stopping when it was at the top of her thighs.

"Want to see more?" she asked.

"Yes," he growled, coming up on his knees as she lifted her skirt higher.

She turned around to reach the zipper that ran down the back of her dress. Then she began to slowly lower it, but he was on his feet to help her.

His breath was hot as he kissed his way down her spine and unzipped the garment. She shrugged her shoulders and the fabric fell forward as she turned away from him and let the dress slip slowly down her body to the floor.

Penny stepped out of it and stood in front of him in just her demi-bra and a pair of sheer black hose. She still wore her stiletto heels and she could tell that Will liked the way she looked. He'd toed his own shoes off and pushed his pants down his legs, along with his boxers. She walked slowly forward, taking her time so that he watched each sway of her hips.

She put her finger in the middle of his chest and pushed him backward until he was sitting on the couch. A moment later, she turned her back to him and bent forward to unbuckle her shoes and slowly slip them off her feet.

He touched her, traced the line of her buttocks and the curve of each cheek. But he didn't stop there; he let his fingers drift down to the backs of her knees and then up between her thighs. She moaned as he rubbed his finger back and forth between her legs.

Penny stepped out of her shoes and pivoted to face him again. She stood there and saw him sprawled out in all his masculine glory, and so in the moment. Turned on by her. She'd never had a man watch her like Will was right now.

A wave of feminine power swept through her. She was responsible for this moment, for making him want her this badly, and it was a heady feeling. She shivered as she slowly removed her stockings, pushing them down her legs and stepping delicately out of them before moving to stand closer to him.

Will kept his hand between her legs, his fingers tracing over her lips, dipping lower to graze the opening of her feminine core. Then he wrapped his arm around her waist and pulled her forward. The feel of him kissing her stomach and pushing his tongue into her belly button was strangely erotic. He nibbled at the skin of her lower belly and then he moved lower. Parting her most intimate flesh with his fingers and flicking his tongue over the exposed bud.

He curled it around and around and then flicked his tongue against her until she spread her legs to offer him greater access to her body.

She moaned and her legs quivered then buckled as he continued to nibble at her clit. He held her up with his arm around her waist, his mouth on her. She braced one leg on the couch and threw her head back as sensation after sensation rippled through her.

She reached for his head, tunneled her fingers into this thick, dark hair and gasped as he drove her higher and higher.

Every nerve in her entire body was pulsing and reached for orgasm. And she put it off, afraid to come before he was inside of her. She wanted to feel that big cock of his stretching out and pushing her over the edge.

Penny pulled back but he tightened his grip on her, maneuvering his body on the couch so he could get better access to her center. He cupped her butt and held her still as he traced his tongue around the opening and then thrust it inside of her. She arched her back, rocking her hips against his mouth.

"Come for me," he said. "Let me see how you look when you come."

His voice was rough and raw and the last bits of her control shattered as he pushed one finger up inside of her. Curling it deep within her as he brought his mouth back to her clit and sucked on it. She felt everything in her tightening, saw stars as she rocked harder against his mouth…and then it happened.

Her orgasm washed over her in a huge wave that left her feeling weak and at the same time so alive. She fell forward against him, catching herself on the back of the couch and in his arms. He wrenched his mouth from her body but kept his finger pumping inside of her.

She felt his free hand rubbing up and down her spine. Felt him flick the fastening on her bra open, and then his mouth was on the curves of her breasts, kissing them as he pulled his hand from her body.

"Are you on the Pill?" he asked.

"Yes," she said. "I'm healthy, too."

"Me, too," he said. "I want inside of you."

"I want that, too," she said. But not yet. She wanted something that every other man had demanded as his due, but this time with Will, she needed to taste him. Wanted to feel that thick cock in her mouth. She shifted so she could stroke him and he stopped her.

"I'm about to come," he said. "I want to be inside of you."

She shuddered as she moved over him and felt the tip of his cock at her entrance. He put his hands on her waist and drew her forward and down on him. It was a slow penetration, each inch coming after the other.

She rocked her hips forward, trying to hurry him, but he gritted his teeth and shook his head. "I want this to last."

"Why?"

"It's our first time," he said, looking up at her with those bright blue eyes of his so intense she felt like he could see all the way to the center of her soul.

She tunneled her fingers through his hair and slowly took him all the way inside of her. Refusing to break eye contact as she rode him with intent.

In her romantic dreams, she and her lover always came at the same time. She knew it was hard to time something like that, but she wanted it. Anticipated that happening with Will. He was so big, filled her so deeply and completely.

He held her with one arm against the middle of her spine as he sucked one of her nipples into his mouth and continued to thrust deep inside of her.

She felt her orgasm coming again. Fingers of sensation spreading out from her center. She leaned forward. "I'm close."

"Not yet," he rasped. "Not yet. You can take more of me, can't you?"

She wasn't sure but then he turned them on the couch, shifted so he was over her, and drove harder and deeper inside of her. And she finally came. Her orgasm rushed over her in waves, and she felt his hips moving faster as he reached for his own release.

He whispered hot, dark, sexy words in her ear as he spilled himself inside of her. The heat of him filling her as he continued to thrust two more times.

He slumped forward, resting his head on her breasts, and she kept her legs wrapped around his waist and stroked his back with her hand.

He felt big and solid. She tightened her arms and legs around him, brushed a kiss against his shoulder and thought, *Mine*.

He was hers. And for now that was more than enough. He'd exceeded her expectations when it came to sex.

"You okay?" he asked huskily, and as he pushed up on his elbows and looked down at her with a soft smile on his face, her heart beat a little faster.

He looked happy and relaxed. His smile was intimate and sweet and it made her crave something that she'd never really thought she wanted before.

And she wanted to hold him to her. Vow that she'd protect the man who smiled that sweetly.

"Yes. Are you?"

"Definitely. Woman, you just about blew every one of my preconceptions of you."

"Did I?" she purred.

"Yes."

She smiled. "Good. I don't like being predictable."

"No chance of that," he said. He rolled them to their

sides, keeping himself inside of her and holding her to him like he didn't want to let go, either.

Their new position put her with her head on his chest right over his heart. She heard the slow and steady beating of it, felt the heat from the fireplace on her back and the slight tickling of his chest hair against her cheek.

She'd never have thought to find this kind of satisfaction with a man. He stroked his hand over the back of her head and down her spine and neither of them said anything for a long time.

But then he shifted on the couch and picked up a blanket off the chair, draping it over her.

He lifted her in his arms and carried her blanket and all to the stairs that lead to the loft bedroom. He set her down on the bed and then opened the curtains so that the stars and moon shone into their room.

"When I was little, I used to think the moon followed me everywhere I went," he said. "You know, we talked about following things… I thought I was so special that the moon always wanted to watch me."

"I like that," she said softly.

"Me, too." He crawled into the bed beside her, wrapped his arms around her and kissed the top of her head. "I've never told anyone else that. Just you, Penny."

Snuggling against him, she realized she had a million questions. She wanted to know what he was feeling and if he usually spent the night with his lovers. When she turned to face him, he was watching her carefully, as if he knew what she was about to ask. She opened her mouth, but he brought his down on hers, kissing her and rebuilding the passion between them. He made love to her again, moving over top of her, and this time they came together. Afterward, she was so exhausted she drifted off to sleep before he pulled out of her body.

She dreamed of flying across the sky in a sleigh with Will and that the world was theirs. That she could have anything she wanted if she had the courage to stop trying to control all the elements and just reached for it.

Then a strong breeze blew, rattling around them, and the sleigh twisted and she fell out. Will reached for her but missed, and she had the feeling that because she was just his temporary lover he simply adjusted his course and kept on moving.

She fell through the night sky, expecting to crash, but fell softly. Nonetheless, she jerked awake with a start.

Will snored softly next to her and she sat there, looking over at him, desperately trying to steady her racing heart. And she realized that as much as she wanted to be cool about this and pretend that she could do temporary tonight, the dream had confirmed that it was going to be harder for her than she'd anticipated.

But she wasn't about to let worry and fear keep her from having the best Christmas of her adult life.

# 8

The next morning he woke to the smell of coffee, and a naked woman pressed to his side. Penny smiled at him through her thick mane of blond hair, which was falling around her shoulders. The sunlight was streaming in through the windows behind them and he caught his breath as she gave him a tentative smile.

"Morning," she said.

"Morning," he replied, taking the cup of coffee from her. He took a careful sip and then sat up and shifted around so he could lean against the headboard.

"I'm not sure what to do now," she admitted. "I've been up for a while thinking."

"What to do about what?" he asked.

"You," she admitted. "Mornings after aren't my forte."

"Why not?" He was intrigued, as always, by each new thing she revealed to him.

"I'm just awkward…and this conversation would be a perfect example of that. It's just hard to know what to do. I don't want to assume we'll do something together and worry that even just asking puts undue pressure on you."

He shook his head as she talked. That was a lot to

dwell on before he even had his first cup of coffee. "Actually, I do want to do something with you today. I picked up a trail map in Fresh Sno yesterday that showed some paths for snowshoeing. And the gal behind the counter said if you go early enough, the snow is pristine and undisturbed. You interested?"

She nodded. "That sounds really nice. What time do you want to go?"

She seemed anxious, like she wanted to leave, and he understood that she might want some time alone to process what had happened last night. God knew he was forcing himself to keep it light and act like nothing had changed, like two weeks was still suitable for him, but deep down inside something had shifted.

She'd seduced him with her body and her soul and he wanted to figure out how he'd let that happen.

He was the one who'd proposed a temporary fling and he was a bit surprised to find his defenses not as strong as he'd hoped. Penny was different. He already knew that. But he'd been confident that he'd be able to conquer that. After all, his own will was strong and he just didn't form emotional attachments the way that others seemed to.

But now he wasn't so sure.

"This morning. What if we both shower and change and meet at the front of the Lodge in an hour or so?"

"That sounds great," she said, jumping out of bed. He was struck again at the beauty of her body.

She was all creamy skin and long limbs. She smiled over at him as she grabbed his bathrobe from a hook by the bathroom door. "I'm borrowing this."

"Okay," he said. "Want to borrow some boots, too?"

"Ah, I see how it is—give you what you want and

now I have to walk back to my chalet instead of being carried."

He got out of bed and scooped her up in his arms. "I haven't come close to getting everything I want from you."

She gave him a serious look from beneath her eyelashes. "What more do you want?"

There it was. The real fear that had her waking him up with coffee and talking a mile a minute before she escaped his chalet.

He didn't know how to answer it. How to give her the response she wanted. To be fair, he didn't have a clue what to say to smooth this over…and that wasn't like him.

He was known for his charm. Known for his romantic gestures. Neither of those would work. Not for her and not this morning.

"Christmas," he said. "A sexy Ms. Claus to spend the holiday with so that when I look back on this year, I'll have no regrets."

She squirmed and he put her down. Then she arched one eyebrow at him. "Sexy Ms. Claus I can do. So you said an hour? I might need a little longer."

"No problem. We have all day and we're on vacation," he said, reminding himself that this was meant to be light and easygoing. But he wasn't sure that suited him any longer.

It didn't take Sherlock Holmes to figure out that he'd disappointed her with his answers, but the fact was, he was simply doing what they'd agreed to.

"Have you changed your mind about this?" he asked suddenly. "I'll understand if you have. My intent was to make sure we both got what we wanted."

Locking eyes with him, she wrapped her arms around her waist. The sleeves of his robe fell over her hands in the process, and she looked small enveloped in it. She kept watching him, searching his face for some sign, and he had no idea what she was looking for.

She said nothing but continued to stare at him. The silence was growing between them.

He tried to look solemn and thoughtful, but imagined he might look odd. So he sighed. "I don't know what you want."

"I don't know, either. I do want to spend more time with you," she said, then lifted her hand to run it through her hair. He watched as the silky strands fell around her shoulders and she tossed her head.

He closed the gap between them, reached for her, but she stepped away and he realized that she was walking a fine line between wanting to be what he needed and needing be what she wanted. It was something he'd seen before but usually at the end of his time with a woman.

"What part was it?" he asked thickly. "What was it that crossed the line?"

She shrugged and looked down at her feet. He noticed the pretty red toenails for the first time. "I don't know. I think it's something inside of me—I should have left last night."

He nodded. "I want to be sure you know that this can't go beyond these two weeks."

She didn't say anything else but walked downstairs and collected her clothing. He watched from the loft as she put on those sexy heels of hers and walked out the door. And in his gut he knew he'd lost something, but he wasn't sure what.

A SHOWER PUT everything into perspective for Penny, plus she had sent a text to Elizabeth and was going to catch up with her friend at the ski lodge while she was having breakfast with Lindsey Collins, the ski pro at the Lodge.

She needed something else to do. To see someone else so she'd stop feeling like Will was her Mr. Perfect. Lesson one: Mr. Perfect wouldn't say, *Let's be lovers for two weeks only.*

Except despite what he'd said, this morning when she'd woke cuddled up next to him, cradled close to his body, it had felt like something more than temporary.

"Good morning," Penny said as she approached.

"Morning. Penny, this is Lindsey. Lindsey, Penny," Elizabeth said.

"Hiya," Lindsey said. "Nice to meet you officially. I think we chatted about that yummy fondue at Elizabeth's promotion party."

"You, as well. Thanks for letting me invite myself to breakfast."

"No problem. We both used to sit at tables by ourselves and one morning we decided to share and chat. And now we're friends," Lindsey said with a smile.

Penny sat down and ordered coffee and oatmeal. She knew it wasn't sexy but she'd always loved it for breakfast and it was healthy.

"You're a guest here?" Lindsey asked in a friendly way. The woman had Nordic good looks and was taller than Penny. She still had the look of an athlete. Penny had watched with the rest of the US as Lindsey took her super-G warm-up run in Sochi and careened off the path into a barricade, sustaining a career-ending injury.

"Yes, but Elizabeth and I were roommates in college," Penny said with a smile. Girl talk. Yes, this is just what she needed. Even at home she didn't have any close friends to talk to since she'd left her job.

"And we've been best friends ever since," Elizabeth said with a wink. She looked so happy and relaxed these days. It wasn't that she needed a promotion or a man to be content, but Penny could tell that having those two things had really helped Elizabeth find her center. "She planned my fab celebration party for my promotion."

"That was a great party," Lindsey said. "I enjoyed it a lot. So thank you for planning it."

"You're welcome. That's sort of what I do for a living," Penny said, taking a sip of coffee and trying to settle into her normal-girls'-brunch mind-set. She could do this. This was what she needed.

"Sort of?" Lindsey asked.

"Yes. I'm between jobs. Do you like being the ski pro?" Penny asked. *Better to keep the spotlight off of me,* she thought. She didn't need to dwell on the fact that her career was as much in limbo as her personal life.

"I do. It's not as rigorous as training was. But I get to ski every day and my knee can handle what I do so it's the best of both worlds." Lindsey cleared her throat, looking slightly uncomfortable. "How are you settling into your new position, Elizabeth?"

Penny noticed how fast the other woman had switched gears, and couldn't help wondering if Lindsey, like herself, wasn't as happy as she was pretending to be.

"It's great. Lars has finally started recovering from his health scare and is relaxing a lot more, giving me a freer hand in management. But I still need his advice. A bigger problem for me is Bradley."

"In what way?" Lindsey asked.

Frowning, Penny added, "Is there trouble in paradise?" She hoped her friends weren't having relationship problems.

"Not at all. But he's pressing me for a wedding date now that we're engaged. I think he wants to get married on New Year's Eve, but I'm not so sure I can plan something that quickly."

Penny thought about it for a moment. It was the kind of project she could use to distract herself from her mono-focus on Will. "I could do it for you. But I need to know what you want. I'm guessing you'd want the ceremony to be small and intimate?"

"Yes, definitely. I think Bradley would be happy with just us and two witnesses."

Penny pulled a notebook out of her bag and started to jot down some notes. "Do you have a venue yet?"

Elizabeth shook her head.

"That's too bad. That could be a challenge for us, especially around the holidays." She chewed thoughtfully on the end of her pen. "But first things first…are you going to take time off or just work and then get married?"

Elizabeth laughed. "Bradley would kill me if I didn't take time off. Do you think you can do this?"

Penny nodded. "I can. Let me know if you want me to."

"I have to check with Lars and the board. But if we do it on New Year's Eve, I think it might be okay. January is actually a pretty slow month for us at the Lodge. Everyone goes back to work after the holidays. Do you think finding a location will be hard?"

"Yes," Penny said, "but not impossible. I've got a little over ten days to plan this. The hardest thing will be to get you a dress."

"I can help with that," Lindsey said.

Penny looked at the former Olympic skier, as did Elizabeth.

"My cousin is a wedding-dress designer in LA. I will call and ask her if she has some dresses in your size."

"Thank you," Elizabeth said. "Ladies, do you really think we can do this?"

"It won't be perfect," Penny cautioned. "I can't work miracles, but I think we can get you a really lovely wedding."

"I think so, too. Bella—that's my cousin—she's always up for a challenge."

Penny was up for one, as well. Something that reaffirmed there was more to life and romance than hot sex and temporary lovers. She needed this. Needed to pour all those emotions that Will stirred to life in her into something constructive so she didn't dwell too heavily on what was missing in their relationship.

*Affair!* she reminded herself. Just a Christmas affair.

PENNY MADE TWO calls before she went to meet Will. The first was to a florist she'd frequently worked with on events back in Maryland to get a recommendation on someone local who could do the flowers for Elizabeth's wedding. The easiest place for Bradley and Elizabeth to have their ceremony was probably here at the Lodge. Given that Elizabeth was the GM, she should be able to find a room or location they could use.

Penny rubbed her hands together and felt that charge of energy she got from planning parties. She loved doing it. She'd forgotten how much over the past few months while she'd been dealing with Butch and quitting her job. He'd tainted something that was a part of her and so personal.

She seemed to have beaten Will to their meeting point; she checked the time on her iPhone and realized that she was about four minutes early. Then she realized she had a call from a number labeled "private number." One without a name. Was it New York?

"Hello?"

"Penny, it's Butch."

"Why are you calling me?"

"Because you won't answer my texts and we need to figure something out. I think if you would just stop being so stubborn…"

"No, Butch. There isn't any way that this will work."

Will walked up as she was talking.

"Please, just listen. I think we had a good thing—"

"We didn't. I've got to go. Don't call me again," she said, hanging up before he could say anything else.

Will didn't say anything, just stood there next to her, and she felt the differences between the two men so clearly. Butch had seemed like he was a solid kind of guy. The type of man who she had a lot in common with, but despite their working together that had been so untrue. And Will, who was so his opposite, had offered her a better relationship.

He'd done it with honesty and no false promises. She realized that he had given her more than Butch ever had. Her former boss had made her believe she might marry him someday when he had already committed himself to another woman. Something that Will would never do.

"You okay?" he asked quietly.

"Yes, much better. I think I was hungry this morning. Must be all that physical activity last night," Penny said, forcing a smile. She was going to enjoy this time with him.

Will Spalding was the man she'd picked to do that with, so no more doubts or wishing for more. Relationships ended all the time and usually long after they had turned to bitterness. This way she'd always have just the good stuff with Will.

"I think I finally get what you meant by two weeks being the best part of the relationship," she remarked.

"You do?"

"Yes. No time for real life to take something special and make it mundane," she said.

He gave her an odd look and she wondered if she were trying too hard to make him think she accepted everything the way it was.

"I can't imagine life with you ever being mundane," he told her.

"Don't do that. Let's not talk about the future, okay? I'm having a really hard time keeping myself from falling for you, Will."

His jaw tightened and he nodded. "You're different for me, as well."

She felt a spark of hope that maybe things would last between them. But then she knew that was false hope. She didn't even know where he really lived or how they would make anything work. And for now, she needed this to be about the two of them and the holiday season. Nothing else.

"So...snowshoeing," she said. "I've never been before, but I read an article in a magazine about it in my room."

"I did, too. That's where I got the idea and thought it might be a bit of fun. Plus with all the snow it seems like staying indoors, while fun for certain things, would be a waste."

"I agree," she said. She needed to keep moving, keep

busy so she didn't have any time to think. "Do you have a vehicle?"

"I rented one from the front desk. A big all-terrain one," he said. "And I had a lunch packed for us. Ready to go and explore?"

She nodded. He led the way to a big Ford Explorer that looked way too big for two people, but given the trail that Will had marked on his map, they might need the all-wheel-drive SUV to get them to the start of it.

"What kind of car do you drive at home?" she asked after she'd climbed up into the passenger seat and he was seated behind the wheel.

"Lamborghini. It was my dream car growing up."

"So you finally made enough to get one?"

"Sort of. I've got my eye on a Tesla electric sports car next. But I'm waiting to make sure they have the bugs worked out of it before I buy one." He shrugged his broad shoulders. "The Lambo is a status thing and I like driving fast. I spend a lot of time online with my investor group and they are all from the Middle East. Those boys have roads where driving over 150 is no big deal. Makes me jealous."

"Why would you want to drive that fast?" she asked, fully admitting to herself that she liked driving under the speed limit when she did take her car somewhere. But most times she was a mass-transit traveler.

"The thrill of it. Makes me feel like I'm alive when I'm going that fast and controlling my car. I'm not dangerous and I'd never want to hurt anyone, but seeing the world flying past my windows always makes me feel like I'm not missing anything."

# 9

It was cold and quiet as they walked through the thick pine forest. He huddled deeper into his coat and looked over at Penny to make sure she was warm enough. She had her head tipped back to stare up at the trees.

The wind shifted and the trees swayed, a large clump of snow falling with a dull thud from the branches. It was nature at its most tranquil. He took his phone out and snapped a picture of Penny with her head back and the thick snow blanketing the ground around her. The only signs of disturbance were the tracks they'd left where they'd been walking earlier.

He wasn't any closer to finding answers about her today. He knew that she was struggling to find her place in the dynamic that had changed between them since they'd become lovers. He was, too.

But they were both ignoring that and acting like they were just in Utah to enjoy themselves this holiday break.

The scent of the pines in the woods made it feel like Christmas to him. Brought him back to the house he'd grown up in. The home he'd had before his parents had died. He'd forgotten about that big pine tree that had been in the foyer of the house and how his mother had asked the housekeeper to put pine boughs in each of the rooms.

He missed his mom.

Will didn't think of her often…but today, when he was standing in the quiet woods with Penny, he wished she were still here so he could talk to her. He had a hunch she'd like Penny. Who wouldn't?

She was beautiful and funny but also very caring. He'd seen the signs more than once.

"Sorry about that. Were you waiting for me?" she asked as she caught up with him. She'd been sort of lagging behind him and he'd let her have her space.

"I was. I wanted to take a selfie," he said, wriggling his eyebrows.

She smiled at him. "I'd like that. It's so lovely out here. I never realized what I was missing living in the city but I like all this rural space around me."

"Me, too," he said. "I live on the outskirts of town on fifteen acres of land so I have it right in my backyard." He wrapped an arm around her shoulders and pulled her up against him, and then stretched his arm with the phone out.

He lifted his arm and Penny moved around, tipping her head from one side to the other.

"What are you doing?" he asked.

"Trying for the right pose. I want to make sure I don't look funny," she said with a grin.

He smiled back and pulled her close, pushing the shutter button as he leaned down to kiss her. She was surprised. He felt it in the way her cold lips parted, but then she sighed as her tongue rubbed against his. She wrapped her arms around his waist as he deepened the kiss and forgot about selfies and preserving this moment. He needed to live in it.

He felt that rush of excitement in the pit of his stomach. A feeling he normally only got when he was making a risky hedge-fund investment or driving his car too fast down an empty highway. And now it was coming from Penny.

He lifted his head and her lips were damp from his kisses, her eyes wide and slightly dazed. He had to get himself under control. Forcing a smile to his lips, he said, "Sorry…couldn't resist."

"Do you hear me complaining? Ready for the photo?"

"Yes," he said and snapped one of the two of them.

"Let's see it," she said.

He showed her the photo and noticed her radiant smile in it.

"Will you send it to me?" Penny murmured.

"I will, what's your email?" he asked. "Weird that we haven't exchanged that info yet. Or friended each other on Facebook."

"I know. But you have a big advantage over all my Facebook friends since we are actually doing stuff together."

He laughed. "True."

She rattled off her email address and he sent the photo to her. "I always loved the smell of pine trees," she told him. "In the winter my mom would buy those Christmas-scented candles and put them all over our house. She tried apple-pie scent but it made us too hungry."

They moved quietly through the trees, following the trail that he'd marked on the app on his smartphone. "My mom used to make the best apple pie."

"Did she?"

"Yes. She didn't do the two-crust thing but instead put some kind of crumble on top of it. It was so good," he said with a smile. "I remember one year, I must have been about six, that my dad and I snuck in and ate the crumble off the pie while my mom was at her bridge club." He chuckled fondly, realizing he hadn't thought of that in years.

Something about Penny brought his old memories up. Reminded him of the power of having a family and how much he'd enjoyed it. He didn't feel that aching loneliness he'd felt in the past when he'd thought of his mom and dad.

"That's funny. Did you get in trouble?"

Will shook his head. "My dad and I left a present for her next to the pie."

"What was it?"

"A bracelet my dad had picked out at the jewelry store and a charm he'd had made from a drawing I'd done of the three of us. Looking back on it as an adult, my dad knew the exact right thing to get her. She loved it."

"Sounds like your parents had a really good marriage," Penny said.

"They did. It was perfect. In a way, again as an adult, I think they would have been miserable if one of them had lived while the other died. They were so connected to each other."

"How did they die?" she asked, slipping her gloved hand into his.

"Car accident," Will said. An over-the-road eighteen-wheeler that a trucker had been driving for too long had swerved. The driver lost control of his vehicle, careening into their path and changing Will's life forever.

"I'm sorry," she said. "But I'm glad you have those happy memories with your parents. Memories are important, aren't they?"

More and more he was coming to realize that.

PENNY ENJOYED THE afternoon with Will. They spotted some fallen pinecones and she picked two of them up to take back to her chalet.

"What are you going to do with those?"

"Just keep them as a little reminder of this outing. I really enjoyed it." She glanced over at him. "I saw a poster in town the other day that said there is a nativity performance on Saturday afternoon. You interested in going?"

"It's not really my kind of thing," he admitted.

"Fair enough," she said, trying not to feel too disappointed. It was a family thing, wasn't it? Watching little kids reenact the night that Jesus was born. Not something that a bachelor who wasn't interested in commitment would attend.

"I have one other event to invite you to and if you don't want to go it's okay. But my friends Elizabeth and Bradley—the cutesy kissing couple, remember them?"

"I do," he said, opening the back of the truck and getting out a thermos. "Would you like some hot tea?"

"Yes, please," she said, taking the insulated mug he handed to her. "They are getting married on New Year's Eve. I'm actually helping to plan it and I wondered if you wanted to make that our last date."

He watched her carefully. "I'd like that."

She imagined he would. It would be a public ceremony and then party, and he could walk out the door at midnight without a backward glance. Or maybe she would. But that was a long ways away. She didn't have to think too much on that right now.

"What's the one thing you have to do for it to feel like Christmas?" he asked suddenly.

She thought about it. Christmas was tied to a bunch of different things that she had to do in order to get into the spirit of the season. "Watch *A Charlie Brown Christmas* some years. Others, it's singing 'Santa, Baby.' And sometimes it's kissing a guy under the mistletoe."

She didn't want to share too much more of herself with him. Spending the afternoon together, hearing about him and his dad eating that pie his mom had baked, it had touched her. Made him even more real than he'd been last night after they'd had sex that first time and she'd seen that tender look on his face. That look that she wanted to see again, but had to be so careful she didn't interpret as anything other than lust.

"I would love to hear you sing 'Santa, Baby,'" he said with a grin.

"I haven't done it since college. My sorority used to put on a show each year to raise money for our charity. And we'd all dress in those cute little Ms. Santa red velvet dresses and sing it." She met his eyes. "I haven't heard that song yet this season."

"I haven't, either. But then I'm not into a lot of the sentimental stuff that is associated with the season."

She wondered if that was because his parents had died when he was young. Parents built traditions for their families. She'd seen that with her mom. Everything that was important to Penny about Christmas either came from her friends or her mom. "So what makes it Christmas for you?"

Will tugged her into his arms and dropped a kiss on

the end of her nose. "This year, you do, Penny. Without you this would be just one more vacation getaway. But you are making it seem very festive."

"Does that mean a different woman each year is how you know it's Christmas?" she asked. No sense lying to herself if that was how he felt. She needed to keep her vision clear and not blurred by sugarplum fairies or snowshoe walks through pine-tree forests.

"Not like you mean it. It's just for me the holiday always starts when I find someone I can share it with."

"So a different girl every year," she reiterated.

A muscle ticked in his jaw as he gazed down at her. "It's not as black-and-white as you make it sound. I have two choices when it comes to Christmas. I can work myself into oblivion and try to miss the fact that most everyone else is celebrating being together. Or I can find a woman who is also a little lost and make the most of that time together until the world sorts itself out and we can both move on."

She took a deep breath. She understood for the first time how much he needed this affair that they were having and how much she sort of needed him, too.

WILL DROVE INTO Park City instead of back to the Lodge and noticed that Penny didn't say anything. He wanted to show her that she was special to him, not like all the others. And as he pulled to a stop in front of the Christmas-tree lot and she turned to him, he thought she was beginning to see that.

"I thought you were getting a tree delivered," she said.

"I am. But I guess I could have two trees," he told her. "I think anyone who likes *A Charlie Brown Christmas* must like going to the Christmas-tree lot."

She nodded. “It’s one of my favorite things to do. I actually haven’t ordered a tree, so unless you really want two of them, we could pick one out for my chalet.”

“Sounds perfect,” he said.

He put his gloves and scarf on before coming around to open the door for Penny. She smiled as she hopped down from the truck and then reached for him and gave him a big bear hug. “Thank you.”

“It’s no big deal,” he said gruffly.

She shook her head and held his hand in hers. “It is to me. Thank you.”

She closed her door and he hit the automatic locks as they walked to the tree lot. There weren’t too many people here at this time of day: middle of the afternoon on Thursday a week before Christmas. Most folks were at work trying to cram in as much as they could before they took off for the holidays.

The two of them wandered through the lot looking at all the trees. “I love this one.” She pointed to a Douglas fir that was full, round and way too tall for their little chalets.

“Might be a bit on the big side.”

“You think?” she asked, laughing at him and at herself. “Just saying I like it. Most of these trees are pretty big. Let’s try over there.”

He followed a few steps behind her, listening to her humming along with the canned Christmas music that played from the overhead speakers. She stopped in front of a tree that was probably only five feet tall and a little sparse. It looked desperately in need of water. Lots of water.

“That’s a fire hazard,” he said.

She nodded. "It is. Reminds me of that pitiful tree that Charlie Brown picked out."

"So that's the one?" he asked, folding his arms across his chest. He doubted that her little dry tree could make it all the way to Christmas day. But who was he to argue with Penny when she was smiling?

"Not sure yet, but it's a definite maybe."

She had shaken the blues or whatever had been dogging her when they'd been in the forest earlier. He wished he could do the same as easily. But talking about his parents was bringing back all sorts of memories—good and bad—and he missed them keenly.

She continued moving through the trees but Will had stopped following her. "White Christmas" was playing over the loudspeaker and the scent of the pine trees brought him back to dancing in the living room with his mom while his dad sang along. It was a happy memory. So then why did his eyes burn and his heart feel heavy?

He wasn't sure how to snap himself out of this. He wondered if he should end this right now with Penny and get on a plane and go to Jamaica. Get his head out of Christmas altogether.

"Hey," Penny said, coming back around the corner and walking over to him. "You okay?"

He couldn't speak. He had promised not to lie and right now there was no way he was going to tell her the truth. He hadn't realized how much of his past he'd shoved away until little bits of it started coming out. Little bits that didn't mean much by themselves, but combined together were shaking him to his core. He had to get out of here.

Had to get away.

He turned and started walking toward the front of

the lot but Penny stopped him with her hand on his arm. "You can't outrun things in your head."

He looked down at her and saw in her eyes that she understood exactly where he was coming from.

"Let's pay for this little tree," she said, "and then we can go back to the Lodge and relax in my Jacuzzi tub and pretend that we both are okay."

"Aren't we?" he asked tersely.

"Let's face it, honey, you and I are both running from something. We don't have to talk about it but we know it. And together maybe I can provide you with a safe place to stop this afternoon. You've done that for me more than once."

She was wise, his Penny, he thought. He walked back to the SUV, carrying her tree, and the lot attendant helped him strap it to the roof before they left. When they got in the car, she put her hand on his thigh and talked to him about things that had nothing to do with Christmas, or family, and it helped.

He couldn't shake it completely, but she was slowly easing that tightness in his chest and that loneliness that was dancing just at the edges. The aching loneliness that promised him that temporary affairs couldn't fill the empty parts of his soul.

She arranged for her tree to be placed in a stand and delivered to her chalet later that evening, after it was watered and trimmed. Then she took his hand, leading him up the path to her place.

Penny didn't say anything, just walked up the stairs to the bathroom with the large garden tub. She turned on the heating and got out some candles from her overnight bag and then turned back to him.

"Ready to relax?"

# 10

PENNY DIDN'T KNOW what had happened at the tree lot but she knew that Will needed a distraction. She ran the water in the large tub and realized he stood behind her, just watching her.

"Would you go downstairs and get the travel speaker from my bag? It's on the end table by my books," she asked.

"Sure," he said, leaving the bathroom. She opened the box of bath amenities that Elizabeth had left for her the first day. There was a lavender-scented bath bomb as well as some bubble bath and those flower petals that dissolved into the water. She found two new fluffy towels and put them on the heated towel rack and then went to retrieve Will's bathrobe from her bedroom. She saw him on the stairs as she came back to the bathroom.

"Thank you."

"For?"

"Not asking questions. Just giving me space," he said.

What else could she do? She wanted to understand this man who was coming to mean more and more to her with each day they spent together, but a part of her knew that she would never fully understand him. That they both had to keep a few secrets from each other in order to survive Christmas with their hearts intact. She could do that. And she promised herself she could help Will do that, as well.

"No problem. It was cold outside today, wasn't it?" she asked.

"Indeed it was. Not too cold though, was it?" he asked.

They were both playing the polite game. She knew that it might bother her later, but not now. "Nope, it was perfect since I knew I had this big tub to come back here to."

"You seem prepared for it," he said wryly.

"It was the amenity that drew me to this chalet. I wanted that big garden tub from the moment I saw it," she said. "I live in a condo and my bathroom isn't the biggest. This year I might have it redone."

"I have a pretty decent-size bathroom with a big shower and that rain-type showerhead." He sighed. "It's heaven. You should think about putting one of those in."

She started to feel normal again. Started regaining her equilibrium and hoped that Will was, as well. She found the matches she'd been searching for and hung his robe on the hook by the door right next to hers.

His was thick and dark blue; hers was thick, also, but a pretty, deep red color. He followed her into the bathroom and she heard him disrobing behind her while she lit the candles and then fiddled with the light switches until just the light over the tub was on.

It was late afternoon but the sky was cloudy and they were forecasting more snow, so soon it would be falling again. She turned the taps off and spun around to find a totally naked Will standing by the sink waiting for her to finish.

"Your turn to get naked," he drawled.

She just smiled at him. She sat down on the bench under the heated towel rack and unlaced her boots, taking them off and setting them next to his. Hers were smaller than his, obviously, but also less worn. She took her socks off next and tossed them on the floor next to his, as well.

Will moved into the tub and sat down along the back, stretching his arms out on either side of his body. He tipped his head back as he sank lower into the water and she almost wished they had a different kind of bond. One where he would be able to share whatever it was that still weighed heavily on his mind.

For herself, she was happy to push that all aside and start to get back to being her. To let go of her fear that she'd made a mistake by sleeping with him. She usually made such bad decisions about men it was hard to believe this wasn't one of them.

She took off her thick sweater, and then her long-sleeved thermal underwear shirt and her bra, before she stood up and began to remove her pants.

"Wait a minute," he said. "Remember when you bent over last night?"

She nodded.

"Would you do it again? I was too turned on and you had those tights on, so I couldn't fully enjoy the view."

"What are you going to do for me in return?" she asked brazenly.

"Whatever you ask me to," he promised. She stood up and pushed her jeans down her legs and off and then walked closer to him, still wearing the thin silk pants that protected her from the cold.

She walked toward the tub and then stopped at the step that lead up to her side. She turned carefully around and glanced at him over her shoulder.

"Like this?"

"Yes. Now lean forward slowly and draw those pants down," he said, his voice getting huskier as he spoke.

She leaned forward as he asked and slowly drew the pants down her legs, and lifted first one foot and then the other to remove them.

She straightened and then slowly drew her panties down the same way. The water sloshed in the tub as he shifted and she felt his wet hand on the curve of her butt as she finished removing all of her clothing. He stroked his finger along her curves and cupped one cheek and then the other. She turned around to face him and he let his finger run along the side of her hip and then the bottom edge of her stomach.

He hooked his hand behind her waist and drew her forward. Dropped a wet kiss on her belly and then reached between her legs to lightly stroke at her center. "Sit on the edge. Put your legs in the tub and sit right here."

Penny climbed into the tub and sat down on the edge as he moved forward between her spread thighs. He parted her with his fingers and she felt the brush of his breath against her intimate flesh before he tongued her lightly. The side of the tub was cold under her backside, but Will was warm and his mouth on her made her forget everything but him.

The way he felt with his broad shoulders between her legs, his mouth moving over her and his arms wrapped

HARLEQUIN
Blaze
NEW YORK TIMES BESTSELLING AUTHOR
Vicki Lewis Thompson
SONS OF CHANCE
Riding Home
Free
HARLEQUIN
Blaze
Command Control
UNIFORMLY HOT!
Sara Jane Stone

Visit us at:
www.ReaderService.com

around her waist, pulling her closer to him—it was pure ecstasy. He flicked his tongue over her and she shivered. Felt her nipples tighten.

Penny pushed her hands into his hair as she arched her back and felt shivers spread throughout her entire body. She was shaking but she wanted and needed more. He pulled her down into the tub on top of his lap. His mouth moved over her torso and licked her nipple. He traced her areola with his tongue and then sucked it into his mouth. She felt the tip of his cock between her legs and reached for it. Stroked her hand up and down his length as he continued to suckle her nipple. The warm water lapped around them and the scent of the vanilla candles she'd lit filled the room.

The jazzy sounds of Wynton Marsalis played in the background but really all she thought about was Will. He was consuming her and making everything—every part of her being—focus on him and him alone. There was something overpowering about him. He pulled his mouth from her breast and scraped his teeth over her nipple before tangling his hand in her hair and bringing her mouth down to his.

His kiss was carnal and raw. She tasted herself on his lips as he shifted beneath her and drove his cock up inside of her. He drove in deep and hard and she moaned against him as she felt the first wave of an orgasm wash over her.

It was powerful and shook her to the core of her being. He pulled out of her and tore his mouth from hers. He was still hard. He hadn't come and she wondered what he was doing.

But he turned her around so that she sat on his lap, facing away from him. Drew her back until he surrounded her with his arms. His cock slid between her legs and he found her opening, thrust up inside of her and then settled down.

"This is nice."

"Nice?" she said, her voice sounded wispy and lost even to her own ears. Her nipples were hard and her entire body felt like it was on the edge again. He moved slowly between her legs, in time with the lapping water but not rushing.

She tightened her core around his cock and he breathed in hard, then bit lightly at the back of her neck. "Not yet. I want this to last."

"I don't," she gasped. "I like the way you make me feel when you move inside of me."

"I like it, too," he said, pulling her farther back against his chest, gently moving around until her head rested on his shoulder. She turned to look at him and noticed that he was looking at her body.

At this angle her breasts were thrust back so that her nipples were exposed to the cooler air and the water surrounded the rest of her. He had one hand stroking up and down the middle of her body. Drawing his finger around and around her breasts and then lower to her belly button. He spread his fingers out and pressed her firmly back against him and the action drove his cock deeper inside of her.

She shivered and shook, so close to another orgasm. She wanted it. She needed it—needed *him*— but this anticipation was making her sensations that much stronger. She didn't want to think about Will, about how much he was rewriting everything she thought she knew about herself. But the truth was, no man had made her feel like this before. She reached her arm back, running her fingers through his hair, and pulled his head toward hers.

She shifted so she could kiss him. Suckle his lower lip and bite it gently. Their tongues tangled together and she felt everything in her body slow. She turned in his arms, straddled him again and took him deep into her. She kept her mouth on his as she rode him hard.

The water splashed around them and he held her waist in his hands, ripping his mouth from hers to call her name as he thrust up inside her and then came in a violent rush. She rocked against him at the same moment, finding her climax seconds after his.

She wrapped her arms around his shoulders and held his head in her hands as she looked into his eyes. They were half-closed but then he opened them and their gazes met and held. She saw in his eyes that he had been moved by this. It was more than sex to him.

Just like it was to her. It was something that neither of them had been searching for. She opened her mouth to ask him about it, but he put his finger over her lips.

"Not right now," he rasped.

"Okay." She settled next to him in the tub, rested her head on his shoulder, and tried to pretend that her Christmas wish hadn't changed from spending the two weeks with Will to keeping him in her heart forever. But she also wasn't going to lie to herself. She knew better than anyone how destructive that could be. She deserved better and so did Will.

He reached for the loofah sponge that was on the edge of the tub, and her scented soap, and then slowly washed her. She let him do it and pretended this would be enough.

PENNY WAS A challenge and every second they spent together made him question things he'd always known about himself. He'd made love to women countless times in the past, but with her it felt new.

Felt like he'd just discovered sex for the first time. He'd just come inside her and he knew that he was ready for her again. Something that didn't happen to him all that often. Granted, he hadn't had sex in almost six months, but he knew it was Penny affecting him and not abstinence.

"Want me to wash your hair?" he asked tenderly.

She looked over at him. "Really?"

"Yes," he said. "I love to play with your hair. It's so soft and pretty. Just like all the princesses from the books my mom read to me as a boy."

"I'm not a princess," she told him. "But I'd love to have you wash my hair."

"Okay. Let me get this set up right," he said, moving to the built-in bench at the back of the tub. "Come sit between my legs."

"Are you sure hair washing is all you have in mind?" she asked with an impish grin.

"For now," he said. He wanted to keep things light and it seemed each time he made love to her, the bond between them grew stronger. He wanted to figure out how to manage his response to her before he took her again.

He cupped his hands and let the water slowly spill out of them down her hair. She closed her eyes and tipped her head back toward his body. He kept pouring water over her until her hair was wet and then he ran his fingers through it. He reached for the shampoo and dispensed some into his palms.

"Lift your head," he said, working the rich lather

through her hair. He liked the way she felt sitting there between his legs, and despite his best intentions, washing her hair was turning him on. But he kept working.

Careful to keep her from brushing his erection as he rinsed her hair, slowly he filled his palms. "Close your eyes."

She nodded and her soapy hair rubbed against the inside of his thigh and his cock, the strands teasing him as they touched him. He poured the water over her hair again and again until all the lather was gone. Then she leaned back and smiled up at him. Her lips were full and pink, her nipples hard and irresistible. He flicked his fingers over them before he kissed her.

"I need conditioner, too," she said, her voice sultry. "Or my hair will tangle."

Will figured she was getting turned on, as well. He liked that. Liked the thought of bringing her pleasure. He wanted to surround her with it so that she'd never forget this or forget him.

He reached for the bottle of conditioner, but she took it from him. Poured it into her own hands and smoothed it through the length of her hair. "You can rinse for me."

After rinsing her hair, he pulled her to her feet, draining the water from the tub. Then he drew her into his arms and kissed her hard and deep. Stepping from the tub and lifting her out behind him, he wrapped a towel around her and carried her to the bedroom.

He put her in the center of the bed, her towel falling open as he came down over top of her. Passion roiling through him, he kissed her deeply as he thrust into her, and he felt her wind her arms and legs around him as he plunged deeper and deeper inside of her.

This time he didn't feel the urgency he'd felt earlier.

This time he made it last, building her to orgasm slowly and enjoying the feel of being entangled in her limbs. When she came, he came with her and then rolled to his side, reached for the edge of the comforter and wrapped them both up in it.

He held her close to him. Too close, because he knew she wasn't his forever and that was something that he was coming to understand that he truly wanted. He never wanted to let her go, but that was what he was going to have to do. He was beginning to fear he wouldn't be able to spend Christmas with her because memories weren't the only thing she was calling to life inside of him. She was also stirring his emotions.

Making him want things he was afraid he couldn't have. Long for things that fate had shown him were just out of his reach. But none of that seemed to matter in this moment. It almost seemed like he was holding everything he'd ever need right here in his arms.

# 11

Penny and Will had fallen into a routine and on December 21—the winter solstice—he suggested they spend the longest night of the year together. First dining at Gastrophile West, the Lodge's five-star restaurant, then dancing in the nightclub, and then going to the second-floor patio bar and watching the night sky.

She had to admit she liked the idea. She'd gotten dressed in a cream-colored velvet gown—she loved wearing velvet at this time of the year—that was discreet in the front with a boat neckline, but in the back it dipped low to the bottom of her spine and the cut-out was lined with two strands of faux pearls.

She started to put on her ridiculously high-heeled shoes but then decided maybe she should wait until she got to the lobby to put them on. The snow was thick on the ground and the skiers had been having a great season on the hills, thanks to all the cold weather. And Penny understood from Lindsey, whom she'd had lunch with the other day, that the snow was just right for perfect conditions on the slopes.

The two women had been working together to plan

Elizabeth's wedding. Since they were both going to be her attendants—Penny as maid of honor and Lindsey as a bridesmaid—Lindsey's cousin was sending dresses for them to try on when she shipped out some wedding dresses for Elizabeth.

Penny put on the pearl earrings her mother had given her as a college graduation present and checked herself in the mirror before reaching for her heavy winter coat. She was having a good time with Will, and the work she'd been doing to plan Elizabeth's holiday wedding had kept her busy enough not to dwell on her secret fears. The ones that only crept up in the middle of the night when she was reminded that she'd only be in Will's arms for ten more days.

*Live in the moment.* She'd been repeating that mantra to herself day after day, and so far she was pretty successful in enjoying her holiday. There were moments when her control slipped, like when she'd been decorating her Christmas tree and Will had brought her a gift ornament of "Fifi." The dog was exactly as she'd described it to him and it had touched her.

It made her realize that he had the potential to be the kind of man she'd want to spend more than two weeks with. The kind of man that, if they'd met under different circumstances, she might have had a chance of convincing that he could be hers forever.

Another part of her thought that maybe he felt so right because it was only temporary. That she was better off cherishing every moment with him instead of analyzing it and trying to change him.

She was reminded of something her mother used to say when she'd been younger: don't worry about tomorrow or today will suffer. Until this Christmas season, she hadn't really understood that.

Penny looked back at her Christmas tree with its beautiful twinkling lights illuminating the darkness of the living room as she flicked off the lamp and prepared to leave her chalet. It was hard to believe, but this little chalet was starting to feel like home. She closed the door and walked up the lighted path toward the Lodge.

She and Will had been careful to balance their time together and apart. The temptation on her end was to spend every second with him, but she knew that wasn't healthy.

Elizabeth was near the concierge desk when Penny entered the lobby. The Lodge was having a special winter-solstice sleigh-ride program, and from the lines Penny noticed in the lobby it seemed to be very popular. She waved at her friend as she headed to the coat check, changed her boots for her high heels and handed in her coat. She kept her clutch with her as she checked her watch.

She had ten minutes until she was supposed to meet Will. She walked through the lobby toward the three-story river-stone fireplace. It was breathtaking as she stood in front of the roaring fire and looked up at the garland decorating it.

She knew every Christmas after this would have a hard time living up to the atmosphere here at the Lodge. It was like she'd stepped into one of those Currier and Ives cards that she'd recalled when she'd gone on her sleigh ride with Will. Everything so picture-perfect.

Even her man, she thought.

Not a detail had been overlooked and she wanted to believe it was real. Wished it could be, but life wasn't picture-perfect, was it? She'd learned that early on when she'd spent all her time with just her mom. Not having that ideal family unit that so many of her other classmates had was hard sometimes, but she didn't begrudge it. Her upbringing had been the best one for her.

And she acknowledged some of those "perfect" families had their failings, as well.

"Penny for your thoughts," Will murmured, slipping an arm around her waist.

"That's my line," she said with a smile, but it was forced. As much as she knew perfection was a kind of lie, she still wanted to find perfect. Wanted Will to be—No. He was her lover for today and she would enjoy it.

"I bet it is," he said. "So what were you thinking?"

"This Christmas is almost perfect. Like an old-fashioned picture with the Lodge and you and me. Just reminding myself not to buy into it."

He nodded. "Are you still okay with everything between us?"

What was she going to say? She wanted the rest of her time with Will, and as much as she was dreading the ending, she wasn't about to do anything that would cut it short any sooner than she had to.

"Yes," she said. Now if only she could convince herself.

THE NIGHTCLUB WAS jam-packed on the fifth floor. The electronic pulse of the music made conversation difficult, but Will pulled Penny closer to him in the banquette. She told him an amusing story about a flopped cake and no dessert at an office Christmas party.

"Sounds like it was fun," he mused. "Do you like hosting parties?"

It seemed like a Penny sort of thing. She was very social. He'd noticed that when they weren't together, he was sequestered in his chalet doing work and she was out and about socializing.

"I do like it a lot. I think part of it is that I grew up with my mom always throwing parties. As a lobbyist, she spends a lot of time schmoozing," Penny said.

"I bet she does," Will added. "My parents liked to socialize, as well. We'd have a big party every year for the Fourth at our estate. They'd invite everyone who worked for the family company out there. It was huge."

And fun. He remembered how hot it would get in Chicago in July. Not Texas hot. He had gone to school in the Dallas area. He wondered if he should tell Penny, find out where she lived now. But to what end? There was absolutely no need for him to know where she lived.

"Sounds like fun. We always did the Fourth in DC. It's so much fun. Makes me feel very patriotic."

The deejay switched from club music to a set of Christmas tunes. They played "Joy to the World," and when Penny closed her eyes and hummed along to the tune, he wondered what memories the song held for her.

He almost asked but then remembered his own caveat. Temporary lovers didn't need to know why. But he wanted to. It made him happy to know all the little details of what made Penny tick.

"You like this song?" he asked when the song finished playing.

"I do. I had a solo one year in choir and got to sing the second verse," she said. "My mom was very proud."

She blushed a little then rolled her eyes. "You know how parents are. Or do you? Did your folks ever get to see you perform in a holiday pageant?"

He rubbed the back of his neck. Maybe the loud music could start up again so he didn't have to answer. But it didn't. He had tried to forget about all those times when he'd been in a show at school and had no one except his butler to watch him. His parents had seen one or two performances, but after they died, that had all ended.

"They saw one," Will said quietly. "We didn't really put on that many shows at my school for parents."

"What was it like to be at a boarding school? Did you miss your home?" she asked. "I'd have been miserable without my own room. But my mom has always said I'm spoiled."

He laughed. "I can see that."

"Hey. A gentleman would have said she was wrong," Penny protested with a big smile.

"I thought we said no lies," he said, winking at her.

"Fair enough. Tell me about boarding school."

He had no idea what she wanted to hear. He'd kept to himself, not because he was ostracized but because his personality had always been more loner than anything else. "I played on the basketball team and tried rowing for one season. We were in double rooms and my roommate was okay. We both just did our own thing and left the other alone."

She took a sip of her seltzer water. He noticed she'd stopped ordering wine after he'd told her about his addiction. "I would have hated that. I probably would have been trying to pester you every time we were alone with questions."

"If you'd been my roommate, I think it's safe to say that I would have been chattier."

"You would have?" she asked flirtatiously. "Do you like talking to me?"

He smiled. "Yes, but as I was a teenage boy, I would have wanted more than conversation."

She nodded. "I remember those days. I'm afraid you would have found me...um...sort of high-maintenance."

"What were you like back then?"

"My mom and I were on our own and she had big dreams for me. I didn't want to take a chance on letting a boy put me off my path." She sighed. "Mom had warned me that love isn't always like it's portrayed in the movies. Sometimes it's difficult and leaves you both a mess."

He leaned back in his chair and studied her for a long minute. In a way he was surprised that was how she felt about love. "Is that why you fall for morons?"

"How did you know that?" she asked. "About the morons?"

"You warned me you were a moron magnet," he said.

"True. Sort of. I think maybe I just got so used to trying not to fall in love that I've never found a man that I could fall for," she said.

He tried not to take that comment personally. After all, he didn't want her to fall in love with him. Except maybe he did. To what end? He had no idea, but he didn't like being painted with the same brush as all the other men who'd been in her life. Deep down he wanted to be the one who finally made her dreams come true.

AFTER LEAVING THE NIGHTCLUB they strolled around the lobby, looking at the display of a model train and Christmas village that was along the south corridor. Penny kept her hand in the crook of Will's arm as they walked. She'd seen that expression on his face when she'd talked of love and she wondered what he'd been thinking.

They both knew that love wasn't an option between

them. Had he changed his mind about ending things between them? Doubtful, since he'd asked her if she was still okay with their arrangement. She dropped her hand from his arm and walked a bit ahead of him as she studied the model train track. She paused to look at the scale replica of the Lodge and leaned forward to pretend she was checking the windows.

But the truth was, she thought she'd caught a glimpse of the man Will might have been if his parents had lived. Because there was great potential in him for love. She saw it—why couldn't he?

She understood that losing his parents had shaped him. She suspected that more than anything was responsible for his attitude toward the holidays and toward longer love affairs. But she didn't know how to change him.

Could she even if she tried? She didn't think so. Will had a strong desire to keep his life on the footing that he'd found for himself.

"I had a train like this when I was a kid," he said. "Come see."

He stretched his hand toward her and she walked back to his side, slid her fingers through his and stood there as the train chugged its way around the track and through the Wasatch Mountains that were depicted around the village. "Look at the steam. It's a replica of one of the old-time trains that first came west. My dad had a huge collection of these up in our attic. It was his hobby room."

Penny listened to him talking and wondered if he even realized that he'd started talking more easily about his parents and his past. She loved each memory he shared with her, understood that he was becoming more and more comfortable with her as he shared these things.

"Did he let you help him with it?" she asked, studying his handsome profile.

"Yes. We were building—"

He abruptly pulled his hand from hers and took a step back from the village. She turned toward him. "What?"

"We had been working on a model of our estate when he died. Dad promised me that we'd finish it when he got home but they never made it back."

His face was expressionless and she knew that he was retreating from her. Pushing his thoughts of his family and the trains down so he didn't have to feel the pain.

"I know that you don't want to remember how he never came home, but what about all the joy you two had working on it? Surely that counts for something," she said softly, walking over to him. She took his hand and led him to the rough-hewn bench that was situated in an alcove near the display.

She sat down and drew him down beside her. Turning to face him, she held his hand loosely in hers and looked into those blue eyes of his. Eyes that she'd seen happy and lusty and determined, but now were walled off.

"There are so many times when I want to pretend that all the bad things that have happened to me, didn't. That they were mistakes that I should shove so far out of my mind that I can never recall them, but I don't do that." She reached up with her free hand and gently stroked his jaw. "Because without all those things—the loser men I dated, the events I planned that didn't go perfectly, the jobs I interviewed for that I didn't get—I wouldn't be here today."

He didn't look away and she thought she might be getting through to him. Saw a softening around his mouth. She wanted him to understand she truly got it. "I still have my mom, so I'm not going to pretend that in any way we are the same, but I think if you remember all the good things, you will see that it makes your life richer."

He nodded. "Thank you. I forget sometimes how blessed my life was. How much they gave me. You're right that I wouldn't be who I am today if that accident hadn't happened." He swallowed hard. "It's just difficult to take the good and the bad, you know?"

She did know. It was so much easier to wish the bad things hadn't happened. But they were the things that truly gave her strength. "Without the bad the good would just be normal and everyday."

"Very true. Thank you," he said, lifting her hand to his mouth and brushing a kiss along her knuckles.

"You're welcome. Do you want to tell me more about the train you and your dad worked on?" she asked.

He shook his head and pulled her to her feet. "No. I think I've had enough of strolling down memory lane for this evening. What do you say we go and make some new memories on this longest night of the year?"

"I'd love to. So far I have to say it's been pretty good. How are you proposing to top it?"

"By taking you back to my place and making love to you. I want to spend the rest of the night wrapped around you and in the present," he said.

She wanted that, too. She kissed him softly and gently because she knew that a part of him was running away again, but he wasn't hers to fix. How many times was she going to have to remind herself of that until the message sank in?

# 12

WILL SPENT THE NEXT morning in Park City, pretending he wasn't hiding from Penny, but the truth was that last night he'd felt raw and exposed. It was one thing to make love to her, quite another to have her see the things that really mattered to him. He didn't know why she was dredging up all the old memories he'd drowned out long ago.

But he couldn't stop thinking of her and of a sort of future for them. Except he knew from his past that there was no way he could make anything like that work. He wasn't good at the day-to-day stuff—he'd had that one brief marriage as evidence—and had no plans to ruin what he had with Penny by making that mistake again.

The streets of Park City were busy and Will almost regretted coming to town today, but he knew that he had to get away. Maybe stay away for more than just the day. In all honesty, he was tempted to drive to Salt Lake City and…leave.

So there it was. The cold, hard truth. Maybe it was time to get out of here if he couldn't really deal with how Penny made him feel.

Will entered a local coffee shop and sat down at a table in the far back corner. He'd brought his laptop with him, and the plan was to distract himself with work and try to get her out of his head. But instead he found himself putting her name into Google search and then reading articles about her.

Yeah, this was helping, he thought sarcastically. But the truth was, he couldn't—or rather wouldn't—ask her about herself, because no matter how screwed up he felt right now, he didn't want to deceive Penny into thinking this could last. But more importantly, he didn't want to hurt her by making her think that he cared more deeply for her than he knew he was capable of.

He rubbed the back of his neck as he scrolled through the articles. There weren't that many but the ones that were there raved about her skills as an event planner. She was at the top of her game. He wondered why the fashion house she'd applied to hadn't already offered her a job.

He sensed sometimes that not having a job for after Christmas was worrying for her. As it would be for anyone. It was hard not to have something to go back to. Was there anything he could do to help her?

He didn't know anyone in fashion. He was about as far from trendy as a man could be, but he did know powerful men who owned big companies that put on a lot of corporate events.

He opened his email and sent a message to the five CEOs that popped into his head first. He mentioned Penny, attached the links detailing her shows and the rave reviews they'd gotten, and then asked them to contact him if they were interested in her.

It wasn't as if this was going to make parting any easier, but it was a gift he could give her, one that she wasn't expecting, and it made him feel good. He hoped it would work out. He knew from the past that coming back from a vacation like this one could be hard. It took time to adjust back to the real world.

"Will…right?" a woman asked, walking toward him.

He recognized the pretty blonde from the resort and thought she was Penny's friend. "Yes, and you are?"

"Elizabeth Anders," she said, holding her hand out to him.

He shook it, wondering where this was going to go.

"Do you mind if I sit here? There aren't any other chairs. I'm waiting for my fiancé so I won't be here long."

"Not at all," he said, pulling a vacant chair out for her at his table. "In fact, I was hoping to meet you, as Penny invited me to be her plus-one at your wedding."

"She did? I'm glad. Penny is doing us such a favor by planning the wedding. I'm not good at being spontaneous."

Will laughed at the way she said it. "Not everyone is. I think weddings planned on the fly can be the best because you don't have time to worry over every detail."

"Are you married?"

He lifted a brow. "Would I be seeing your friend if I was?"

"You never know."

"Well, I'm not. But I was a long time ago. And my bride was the biggest, most badass bridezilla to walk down the aisle."

Elizabeth laughed. "I'm not like that. *I hope*. I did have a short list of things that I wanted to make sure Penny included, but I left the rest to her. Did she tell you we were roommates in college?"

He realized he had a chance to learn more about

Penny, more than he'd find out on the internet, from Elizabeth. He had a twinge of conscience about it, but then shrugged it away. His intent wasn't to use the information for nefarious purposes. He just wanted to know more about the woman he cared for.

"No, she didn't mention that," he said. "What kind of roommate was she? She said she likes to *chat*." Elizabeth laughed and nodded at him. "She does. But she's the best at cheering me up when I'm down. I have a real desire to be the best at everything—it's a big flaw, I know—but when I'd get a bad grade or not be in the top one percent in our class, Penny would bake me cookies and sit on my bed and talk to me until I didn't feel bad anymore."

That sounded like Penny. She had a sunshiny personality and he wondered why she hadn't found a better man to love. He knew she'd said that she had wanted to wait to find a good man, but surely it was time for that.

And as much as he hated the thought of her with anyone other than him, he wanted her to be happy.

THE DRESSES THAT Bella sent for Elizabeth had been sent to her home, but she'd included three bridesmaids' dresses each for herself and Lindsey to try on. Penny opened the package and realized they were all gorgeous. She took them out of the box slowly and held them up to herself.

Not for the first time, she had to admit she was both happy for Elizabeth and a little envious of her, as well. She'd met a great guy, overcome her problems, and now she was getting married. As opposed to Penny, who had met a great guy and agreed to have a two-week affair with him.

She turned away from her mirror and tossed a dress

on the bed. She was a mess. She did a good job of pretending that she was dealing well with everything that was going on in her life, but she didn't have a job, her boyfriend was leaving her on December 31, and unless she got her act together, she wasn't going to be able to keep fooling her friends that she was okay.

She went downstairs to the refrigerator and opened the freezer section, taking out a pint of Ben & Jerry's ice cream, and then got a big spoon. She needed the kind of comfort that only Ben and Jerry could provide. Christmas music was playing, except right now it was a sappy ballad about New Year's Eve. She walked over to her smartphone and skipped the song. What she needed was something loud and cloying, something like "Rudolph the Red-Nosed Reindeer," not something romancey. Nothing about love or plans for New Year's Eve.

The last night she'd have with Will.

She sat down on the couch, tossed the lid to the ice cream on the table and went in for a big spoonful. But it was frozen. Like, really frozen. So damned hard she couldn't get the spoon into it.

Just her luck, she thought, fighting back tears.

She put the container on the table as the songs changed again, and "I'll Be Home For Christmas" came on. She just went ahead and flicked off the music. Silence would be better than songs that stirred too many emotions inside of her.

She knew she could do this. Her own mother was in the Caribbean having the Christmas of her life with her new husband. She was glad Will hadn't asked why she wasn't spending the holidays at home, because the truth was, she didn't have one right now. Once her mom and Peter had settled into being married maybe she'd go home for holidays, but not this year.

Instead, she was standing in front of a Christmas tree decorated by her and the first man she'd really cared for in a long time.

She knew she was close to falling in love with him. It was hard not to. He did all the right things. Said all the right things. Let her be herself and just got her.

She hugged the throw pillow from the couch to her stomach. She was losing it. She'd been doing so well but planning a wedding for her friend was stupid when she was with Will. It made her think of things she normally ignored. Like if she were planning her own nuptials she'd make sure they were married outdoors in the summer in a park. Because she knew he liked to be outside and she liked the idea of it.

She had been scanning wedding magazines for ideas so she didn't forget anything for Elizabeth, but she'd ear-marked pages with things she'd want for herself. It was ridiculous—she knew it. But all the same, she couldn't really help herself.

She looked at her pint of ice cream and noticed that it looked softer. She picked up the container and took a big scoop before heading over to her laptop to look for a Christmas present for Will. She had to get something for him. She thought about it for just a minute, and knew her idea could be something that he'd either love or would really be upset by. But she wanted him to have the train that reminded him of his childhood.

On top of that, she wanted to give him something that would resonate with him long after he'd forgotten her. Which he would. Just like she knew that eventually she'd forget him. Or would she? She hoped she would. It would be easier to keep on pretending she loved being single and free if she didn't remember this time with him.

Penny placed her order and asked for overnight shipping and then got up from the computer. She was going to do something for herself now—not Elizabeth or Will. Like maybe baking a big batch of cookies and taking them to the homeless shelter that Elizabeth and Bradley volunteered at.

She liked that idea. It would serve her well to remember how good she had it. That her life was filled with sweet blessings and she was standing in the spot that she'd carried herself to. And even though she didn't want to say goodbye to Will, she had to remind herself often that this was what she'd originally wanted. A no-strings, red-hot Christmas affair so that she could go back home in January and start with a clean slate.

She just hadn't realized back then that she'd have such a drastic change of heart. That was sobering, but as she mixed up a double batch of her hazelnut chocolate-chip cookies and baked off ten dozen of them, she started to find peace inside herself again.

WILL THOUGHT HE saw Penny in town at the homeless shelter and followed her inside. "Wait up."

She turned toward him with a large box in her hands that had the Lodge's bakery's logo on it.

"What are you doing here?" she asked.

"I've been in town all day, trying to get some work done," he said. When he was at the chalet he saw Penny everywhere and it made him horny—not really the right mind-set for work.

Not that he'd been able to be very productive today, anyway. It had been enlightening talking to Elizabeth and he realized as she'd shared stories about Penny how much he cared for her already.

"Did you get a lot accomplished?" she asked.

"Not really. But on one project I learned a lot more." He gestured toward the box. "What have you got there?"

"Cookies. I was making myself a little crazy with wedding planning, so I decided to bake and now have ten dozen cookies."

He laughed. Weddings were a woman thing that he would probably never understand. But he got that they were important to some of them. "Are there more cookies in your car?"

"Yes. It's the SUV we rented the day we went snowshoeing," she said, handing him the keys. "Would you mind helping me?"

"Not at all," he said, taking the keys and leaving her to talk to the man who ran the shelter. He grabbed the remaining two boxes from the backseat and carried them carefully across the icy parking lot. He had spent the entire day trying to get some distance from Penny, but it seemed the harder he tried to keep her at arm's length, the closer she got to him.

He knew that she wasn't trying to do anything to bind her to him but it was happening all the same. Maybe it was because she was being so careful to not ask too many questions about his past. She seemed content to let him share the memories that he wanted to. But perhaps that was part of her plan.

Except he found it hard to believe that the woman who'd baked ten dozen cookies for the homeless of Park City had an evil plan to make him fall for her. In fact, logic said that the opposite was true. That he was falling for her because she *didn't* have a plan. Some of the women he'd dated in the past had played at being happy with a temporary affair, but with Penny, he knew that she'd really just wanted that in the beginning.

He wouldn't blame her if, like him, she'd found her feelings changing. It was hard to spend as much time together as they had and not start caring.

Releasing a ragged breath, Will wondered if he'd finally found the one thing that would make it hard to live up to his own promises to himself.

"Where should I put these?" he asked her.

"Follow me," Penny said. She was wearing a pair of tan-colored leggings that hugged her shapely legs and a pair of riding boots that ended just above her knees. She had a light blue sweater on that ended midthigh with a big cowl collar. Her blond hair was braided to one side.

She looked cute. Tempting. It was hard to keep his mind where it needed to be when she looked like that and stood close to him smelling of vanilla and yummy cookies.

He was only a man after all.

He put the cookies on the counter where she gestured for them to go and then he turned toward her. She smiled sweetly. "I sort of missed you today."

"You did?"

"Yes, but don't let it go to your head." She looked up at him. "I had already talked to Mr. Peabody about helping out tonight. Would you like to stay as well? He said the closer it gets to Christmas, the busier everyone is."

He nodded. "I'd enjoy helping. Do you do this often?"

"At home I try to go down to the shelter there at least once a month, but today I was feeling sorry for myself and needed a reminder of how good my life is."

He smiled at her. He doubted that she moaned too

much about her life—that would be anti-Penny. As the thought entered his mind, he knew he had to end this. He was getting in way over his head. His life had worked for him because he hadn't let anyone become too important to him, but already he could tell that she was. That Penny was the one woman he didn't want to have to leave.

He stood next to her, helping serve food to the homeless who came through. Talking to them as they came up with their trays, he realized that some of these people could really use his help. So instead of listening to Penny's chat with the family who were the last ones in line, Will went out to the dining room and sat down at a table with six guys and started a real conversation with them.

He found out a little about each of the men, the kind of work they'd done and how they'd ended up here. Then he talked about his own struggles with alcohol, partly because he knew from the AA meetings he'd attended in the past how helpful it was to learn that someone else was walking in your shoes.

"I had to start completely over with my career after I got out of rehab the last time. And I couldn't have done it without the help of a mentor. Here's my card in case any of you need any help getting back into the workforce."

He sat there nursing a cup of coffee until Penny was done, but when he looked up to find her, he noticed she was leaning against the wall near the door watching him. Slowly, the place cleared out and he walked over to her.

"Why are you looking at me like that?"

"Every time I think I know you, you surprise me."

# 13

THE SOUND OF sirens jerked her from a solid sleep, and she glanced around her bedroom. She was alone. God… was Will all right? She heard the loud, shrill wails growing closer, so she hopped out of bed, grabbed her robe and ran downstairs. Everything was okay in her unit. She shoved her feet into her UGGs and opened the door, sticking her head out.

The sirens were much louder with the door open, and she looked up toward the Lodge, where she saw a fire truck. She glanced at Will's chalet and saw him hurrying toward her in his robe and boots.

"Are you okay?" he croaked.

"Yes. You?"

"I'm fine," he said, reaching out and wrapping her in his arms. "Thank God you're all right. I was so worried. I should have stayed at your place tonight in case you needed me."

She hugged him close. "No more sleeping apart."

"Agreed," he said. "We only have a little over a week left together."

"I know," she murmured as she tilted her face up to

gaze into his eyes. He didn't have to remind her of how much time they had left—she'd been keeping close track of it in her mind. Although she'd been trying to keep herself from caring more deeply for him, to make their eventual parting less painful, it was virtually impossible to let her mind control her heart.

So why waste precious time fighting a losing battle?

"Will, I don't want to worry about you when we are apart," she said.

He kissed her long and hard, and in that kiss she heard and felt all the things that she believed he couldn't say. That he'd been scared for her and didn't want to be alone again.

He swept her up into his arms and strode toward her chalet. She'd left the door open and he carried her over the threshold and closed the door with his foot. She leaned down to lock it.

"I'm staying tonight."

"I know," she whispered.

"Just wanted to make sure there were no doubts," he said. "I don't think I can sleep without you in my arms."

He walked to the couch and sat down, cradling her on his lap. Her Christmas tree lights were the only illumination in the room. They heard the sirens stop. Penny hoped everyone was okay at the Lodge and wondered if she should contact Elizabeth. But she knew there was nothing she could do right now.

"Want some hot cocoa?"

"Yes," he said. "I'll make a fire."

She got off his lap and went into the kitchen area, then warmed some milk before melting chocolate in it and pouring it into two mugs. She heard her phone beep upstairs and Will looked over at her.

"Want me to go get your phone?" he asked.

"Yes, please. I'm worried about Elizabeth."

He ran up the stairs and was down a moment later. "It is from Elizabeth. Sorry, I didn't mean to read it, but it was on the screen. I met her in town yesterday. She's nice."

"She's the best. Is she okay?"

"Yes. Why don't you read her text?" he said, handing her the iPhone, "and I'll bring the mugs over. Too bad you don't have any more cookies."

"Well, we can bake some tomorrow. We'll need some to leave out for Santa," she said.

"What's that?"

"My mom always had me put out cookies for Santa, and now it's become a habit I can't quite break."

He smiled over at her as he poured milk and found the bag of marshmallows she'd left on the counter. She'd bought them when she'd been in town because Will had mentioned that he liked them in his cocoa.

"Where is your mom this Christmas?" he asked curiously.

"In the Caribbean with her new husband. She got married last July," Penny said.

"You don't spend the holiday with her?" Will asked.

"No, not usually. But that's because a lot of years she's working or I'm working. Last year, I had planned a big party that was for the families of our biggest sales winners. I didn't work on Christmas day, but the party was on December 24 so it made sense to just stay home instead of traveling. Mom and I go on vacation each February."

Penny skimmed the message from Elizabeth, which simply said that the resort fire alarm had been pulled and that they'd taken care of the problem, and she hoped that Penny was okay. Penny texted back that she was fine and sat down on the couch as Will brought the mugs over and settled down next to her.

"Why do you go on vacation in February?"

"It's silly but mom and I are usually single, so we get out of Dodge for Valentine's Day. Most of the time we go someplace we haven't been before. Last year it was Venice."

"It doesn't sound silly at all. I do the same thing, except it is more of a staycation in my house. I don't leave it for days." He grimaced. "It's impossible to go to a store, even the gas station, without being bombarded with all those hearts and flowers."

She took a sip of her cocoa and leaned her head back against the sofa. She had a feeling this year her mom might not want to go away. And she was thinking about her clean slate and her future and it didn't look as great to be starting over in January as she'd thought it might.

She was going to miss Will, true. That he was there for her in the middle of the night and whenever she needed him.

"What am I going to do with you, Penny?" he asked.

*Love me,* she thought. But she knew that wasn't the answer he was looking for. She surprised herself by thinking it. "Enjoy Christmas with me."

ENJOYING HIS TIME with her was becoming harder and harder. She stirred too much inside of him. Things he never wanted to feel or think about again. And he knew that no matter how much he tried to keep things from going any deeper, it was almost too late.

If he were a different sort of man…then maybe this

could work, but he wasn't and she couldn't change him. He drank the cocoa she'd made and remembered that he'd been sleeping at his place to preserve the distance he needed between them.

But waking up to an alarm, fearing something could have happened to her, had brought home to him that no matter what the future held, at this moment he needed her close to him. Needed to ensure her safety and well-being.

She seemed pensive and not her usual sunny self tonight. He toyed with a strand of her hair as she leaned back against the couch and sipped at her drink.

"Thanks for getting marshmallows," he said.

She shrugged. "It was no big deal." But he knew it was. She'd gotten them for him. It was the kind of small gesture that let him know she thought about him when they were apart.

"Actually, I'm lying," she confessed. "I've been thinking about you a lot and I like doing things that make you happy. But my intel on you is kind of limited, and I'm struggling not to ask too many questions or try to get to know you better."

"Why?" Will asked in a low voice. But he wasn't ready for this conversation. He'd thought they'd have at least until the day after Christmas before she started realizing how close they were to leaving each other.

"Because then it will be harder to say goodbye. I'm not going to try to change our agreement, but I can't tell if it's because we know when it will end that I find you so attractive…or if it's the real thing."

Will felt the same but there was no way he was going to let her know. He needed to keep her in the dark about his feelings so that he could continue to lie to himself. "Hell."

He stood up and walked over to the window that overlooked the Wasatch Range. It was dark and he saw only a shadow of his own reflection in the glass. He looked like a man who'd spent too long running.

But he couldn't stop. Wouldn't stop. Already Penny was making him confront things he'd thought he'd left in the dust.

"I'm not going to say I'm sorry," she said. "That would be a lie. But I will say I didn't mean to feel this way."

He turned to face her. She had her arms crossed around her waist and watched him with that level stare of hers that made him feel like he'd let her down. Hell, he knew he had. He'd let himself down, as well.

"Penny, I can't. There are too many things in my past that I just can't share with you. You have helped me recall some happy memories of my childhood that would have been lost forever, but there are other things that I don't want to relive. I can't do it. I'm sorry."

He didn't want to end things now. He wanted it to be like the Christmas song. "We are close to having a merry little Christmas," he said. "Penny, put your troubles away and let this continue the way it has been."

"I'm trying, Will. Really, I am. But it's hard. I want to know all about your past. I want to share things about mine. When you asked about my mom, it occurred to me that she'd like you. And I think you'd like her." She sighed. "But that's not what we are about, is it?" Will watched her carefully. He knew she needed more from him, and he had this moment. This one chance to buckle and give her what she needed, but he was afraid he'd just be fooling himself if he did that. Every relationship he'd had ended. First the one with his parents—he knew that was an accident but they were gone. Then his brief marriage had sort of cemented the fact that he didn't know how to make something last. He wanted to believe things would be different with Penny, but he wasn't sure that they really could be.

Because no matter how much it might seem as if the two of them could build a meaningful life together—away from the Lodge—he feared that was just a fantasy. Before long, the real world would intrude, and he'd end up breaking both their hearts.

Frustrated, he raked a hand through his hair. "Do you want me to leave?"

"No," she said. "I want you to care."

"Dammit, I do care, Penny. Don't think that I don't."

"Then why is this enough for you?" she asked, waving her arms around. "Just two weeks? That's not healthy."

"It is healthy. And it's all I have to give you. It's okay if you've changed your mind," Will said, but in his heart he knew it wasn't. He wasn't ready to say goodbye to her yet—he wanted all the days she'd promised. Those hours belonged to them.

"I haven't changed my mind," she informed him. "Maybe I've changed my heart. I thought I would be safe by knowing we were going to say goodbye on December 31, but I'm not. I care about you, Will. Each and every hour we spend together makes me want to hoard them in a memory chest."

She turned away and walked to the kitchen, putting her mug in the sink before she faced him again. She braced her hands on the counter and leaned over to stare at him. He thought he saw a sheen of tears in her eyes and he knew a better man would leave, end it now before this went any further, but he was also a little selfish and he wanted her. Needed her.

"Should I go?" he asked again.

Penny said nothing. Just kept watching him. Then she shook her head. "No, I don't want that. I want—" She broke off and shook her head. "Never mind…I'm fine. I think the fire alarm just scared me because I was afraid for your safety."

"I understand that," he said, coming over to her, rubbing his hand over the back of her head to see if she'd let him touch her.

She turned to face him and then sighed and curled her arms around him. He held her loosely but inside the vise around his heart loosened as they embraced. He was afraid he'd lost her.

PENNY HAD PUSHED and hoped for better results, but at the end of the day—or in this case in the middle of the night—she didn't want to say goodbye to him. He smelled so good and she felt safe in his arms. He threaded his fingers through her hair, tugging gently until she tipped her head back.

He brought his mouth down to hers. Kissed her long and hard, their tongues tangling as he thrust his deep into her mouth. He lifted her off her feet and set her on the countertop. She cradled his face in her hands and leaned down to keep kissing him.

His hands slipped inside of her robe and caressed her body through the thin layer of her nightgown, and she wrapped her legs around his middle.

He tore his mouth from hers and looked up at her.

"Is this enough?" he bit out. "Please let this be enough for tonight."

She swallowed. She wasn't about to say no. Not to-night. "Yes."

He lifted her in his arms again and carried her up the stairs to the bedroom. The music continued to play downstairs and the lights from her tree were the only illumination. He let his robe fall to the floor and he was naked underneath, and obviously turned on. She reached for him. Touched his smooth chest with that thin smattering of hair that went down his abs.

She let her fingers explore him and he stood there with his breath catching in his throat as she brought her hand closer and closer to his erection. He was such a fine male. She felt lucky to have found him.

She wrapped her hand around his cock and walked backward to her bed, tugging gently, but he was right in step with her. She stroked him up and down, reaching between his legs to cup his balls.

She wanted this night to force him to realize how much she meant to him. To make this night one they'd never forget. She wished there was something she could say that would make him start thinking about staying with her for longer than the end of the year.

But for right now, she needed to have him inside her. To feel him possessing her…body and soul. She needed to reaffirm that her grasp on him, however tenuous, was still there.

He kissed her again and she saw in his passion-glazed eyes that he wanted to say something, but she felt like she was on the edge of losing it and just couldn't talk anymore.

Penny slid her robe off her shoulders and sat on the edge of her bed, scooted back until she was in the middle, then pulled her nightshirt up and over her head and threw it on the floor.

"Make love to me," she said. To her ears, her voice sounded raw and strained, but she didn't care. Hiding the fact that she wanted him was beyond her. Tonight she'd laid her cards on the table and she'd lost.

*Lost.*

God, she felt adrift, and the only thing that she was sure of was that she wanted him to make love to her until she could stop thinking. Otherwise she'd never be able to sleep and she'd have to do the one thing that she really didn't want to.

Say goodbye to Will.

But she wasn't going to let this be the end. She was going to prove to Will in any way she could that there was still more between them.

He walked forward and put one knee down on the bed and then crawled toward her.

"Penny—"

"Don't say anything. I just want sex," she said.

His eyes said he knew she was lying, but he stopped talking and came up over her. Used his chest to caress her from the apex of her thighs to her breasts, and then his mouth was on hers as he propped himself up on an elbow and stroked her from neck to waist and back again.

She was swept up in the passion, kept kissing and caressing him. Needing to memorize his entire body with the touch of her hands. She wouldn't stop. She needed him. Needed him *now.*

She reached between his legs and grasped his cock again.

He moaned her name and the sound sent shivers down her spine. The way he made love to her always made her believe that he must care deeply for her, but then she remembered that he was good at compartmentalizing things. Including women. Especially her.

"Are you ready for me?" he rasped.

"Yes," she said.

He shifted his hips and she felt him at the entrance of her body. He pushed forward slowly, just an inch entering her.

"Take me hard," she commanded.

He groaned and thrust all the way into her. Penny moaned his name, and as he continued to pound into her, she threw her head back. She wanted to keep him there. Keep him in her bed and in her body since he wouldn't allow her to keep him in her heart.

She stroked her hand down his back and cupped his butt, urging him to ride her harder and harder until her orgasm took her by surprise. She came hard, stars dancing behind her eyes and her breath rushing out of her in quick gasps.

He came a second later and collapsed on top of her, his body covered with sweat and his hot exhalations brushing over her breast. He pulled her close for a cuddle and she thought about turning away. Making him leave. But she knew that would be spiteful and she wasn't going to sleep without him by her side just to prove to herself that she could. Come January 1 she'd be sleeping alone every night.

That would be soon enough.

# 14

WILL DIDN'T SLEEP WELL. His dreams were plagued by fires and Penny. He was the one trapped inside and he couldn't get to her no matter how hard he tried.

He sat up, scrubbed a hand over his face and looked at the empty bed. Where was she?

He listened carefully but there were no noises from downstairs or the bathroom. Getting up, he pulled on his robe and went downstairs to find a note telling him that she had gone to meet her friends for breakfast and that he could let himself out.

She'd signed her name and added a little smiley face after it, but in his gut he knew that nothing was the same this morning.

He had let her down last night. Or maybe she'd let herself down, he couldn't say for sure. But something had changed between them.

He found his boots and put them on and then left her chalet for his. His Chrismas tree was arriving today and he'd asked her to dinner, but he wondered if she'd still show up. It was December 23. Only two more days until Christmas and a part of him wanted…to slow time.

But the other part, the realist inside him, wanted it to go more quickly. Needed to find a way to get her out of his life before she found her way deep into his soul. God, what a mess.

He entered his chalet, showered and changed, and then sat down at his computer. Work, which had long been his shelter from loneliness and his messed-up life, wasn't working. Instead, as he read the financial pages of various international newspapers, he was struck by the fact that none of the CEOs he'd written had gotten back to him about a job for Penny.

Dammit. She mattered to him. Really mattered to him.

What was he going to do? Maybe start pulling back. Make up excuses—lie? It was the one thing he'd promised her he wouldn't do. The one thing that he knew was the unbreakable promise between them. He was aware of how her last lover had deceived her. Understood why lying wasn't something she'd tolerate. And normally he'd agree, but in this instance, it might work in his favor. Give him the clean break he needed.

Because she had become too important to him.

If he thought there was a chance in hell that they could continue on, he might be tempted to take it. But he didn't believe in forever. Had tried it once to disastrous results. He knew that he wasn't like other folks. Or maybe that he was like the 50 percent of people who never could commit to someone else.

He'd felt superior to the men that had been in Penny's life before. Had told himself that he was better than they were, but now he felt like a total fraud. That by offering her this temporary affair he'd proved he was just the same as the others.

He wanted to be better. Wanted to give her everything but was too aware of the failings inside of himself. Things that made it impossible for that to happen.

Will left his chalet, but instead of heading toward the Lodge, he started down the path that lead to the hiking trails. He needed to clear his head. The air was cool and as he walked away from the Lodge and civilization and the signs of Christmas that were everywhere, he felt his pulse start to calm and that inner peace he worked so hard to keep returned.

This wasn't a "make it or break it" moment in his life. She was just a girl.

No, she wasn't. She was Penny. She had that thing that made him want to be better and to stay in the sunshine that she projected with her smile.

He stopped walking and sat down on one of the benches the Lodge provided. His legendary cool had deserted him and he had a sinking feeling that he wasn't going to get it back by running away from her.

But staying?

He hadn't lived with anyone since he'd tried marriage. Kara had lasted for exactly six weeks before she'd ghosted out of his life. Rightly so. He'd been…obsessed and controlling.

He knew how he got when a relationship was serious. It didn't matter that he'd been twenty-one then and in desperate need of someone to call his own.

At thirty-five he still wanted that and didn't like it. He didn't have that thing that other men did that made them normal in a relationship. He knew how he could be, and by adding the word *temporary*, he'd found a way to keep things from getting out of hand. To have companionship for a short time without losing himself.

Or scaring off the women. In this case, Penny.

He got up and started hiking again, but no matter how fast he walked, he couldn't outrun his past. Couldn't get the image out of his head of making an offer to keep her in his life only to have it ruin them both.

He needed to remember that Penny was different and special, but she wasn't meant to be his forever. He couldn't forget that.

Will heard the silence of the trees around him and the sound of the snow falling from the branches. It reminded him of the snowshoeing he'd done with Penny. He really wasn't sure how he was ever going to be able to be free of her.

Already he wanted her more than anyone else. And the feelings he'd had for Kara at twenty-one seemed like mere puppy love compared to the depth of need he now had for Penny.

He started running instead of walking. Felt the burn of each inhalation of cold air down his throat and into his lungs. He ran faster and found a pace that was punishing, and since the path was icy and uneven in places, he had to pay attention. Will did it for as long as he could and then slowed to a walk to cool down.

He put his hands in the pockets of his jacket and found a piece of paper he hadn't realized was in there. He pulled it out. The note from Penny that morning. He traced his finger over her signature and her smiley face, and knew he wanted to be the one who kept her smiling.

BREAKFAST WITH THE girls had never been so welcome. Elizabeth had picked both her and Lindsey up at the Lodge and driven them to her house. She and Lindsey brought the bridesmaids' dresses that Bella had sent them. The plan was to try everything on and pick a dress that morning.

Penny sat in the backseat, staring at the landscape as they drove to Elizabeth's house. The last thing she wanted to do this morning was talk. Last night she'd realized she couldn't keep lying to herself and pretending that temporary with Will was okay. She'd vacillated back and forth over the course of the days they were together, but she knew now she couldn't keep doing it.

She really cared for him—borderline loved him. She didn't want to admit that or let herself care that deeply, but she faced the fact that it might be too late.

"You okay?" Lindsey asked when they were in Elizabeth's house and her friend had gone into the bedroom to try on the first wedding dress.

"I'm fine…just tired," she said. "There was a fire alarm in the middle of the night at the Lodge."

"I heard about that from the staff at the recreation area. I'm glad no one was hurt."

"Me, too."

"I need help doing the back of the dress," Elizabeth announced, walking into the living room. The dress was in the art-deco style, which Elizabeth loved. It was made of white satin and skimmed close to her body at the top, gently flowing outward through the skirt. The neckline had very stylized platinum embroidery. She stood there in front of them with her hair flowing around her shoulders, and Penny thought she was absolutely stunning.

She hurried to help her friend do up the gown. The simple design showed off Elizabeth's own effortless beauty. Made her the one everyone wouldn't be able to take their eyes off of. It was a little big in the bust but otherwise fit like a dream. The bride's mom was coming into town tomorrow and would handle the alterations. They were trying the dresses on in Elizabeth's living room because she had a panel of mirrors on the wall. Her friend turned to look at herself and Penny knew from that sparkle in her blue-green eyes that she liked what she saw.

"I love it," Elizabeth said. "There's a veil to go with it. Will one of you go get it? It's sort of a cap with a long veil."

"I'll do it," Lindsey offered.

Penny hugged her friend and felt the stirring of tears at the backs of her eyes. "You look so gorgeous. Bradley isn't going to be able to take his eyes off you."

"It's perfect. I couldn't have picked something more me."

"Here ya go," Lindsey said as she rejoined them. The Nordic blonde helped Elizabeth get the veil on her head and adjusted the long train of her dress and then just stood next to the bride-to-be.

"Okay, that's my dress," Elizabeth said. "Now what about you two?"

"Um, I liked the red and green colors. So I had a thought…" Penny began.

"I like the green one best," Lindsey interjected.

Elizabeth looked at her best friend. "What's your thought, Penn?"

"What if I teamed the dresses with some gray snow boots for the outdoorsy photos?"

"I love it," Elizabeth said.

"Me, too," Lindsey added.

"Go try the dresses on," Elizabeth urged, and they both went to separate bathrooms to get dressed and then came back.

Lindsey looked so tall and graceful that Penny felt like a little kid standing next to her. But at least the dress she'd been sent fit her pretty good since they'd sent their measurements to Bella and she'd gotten even the skirt length right.

"You two look beautiful," Elizabeth said, wrapping her arms around each of their shoulders and drawing them close to her.

Staring at the three of them in the mirror, Penny smiled. They did look good. "I like it."

"I do, too. That was easy," Lindsey said. "My sister took four weeks of dress shopping before she ended up picking the very first dress she tried on."

"That's crazy…and since I only have a week until the wedding, I can't be too picky. Plus this is lovely. Bella really paid attention to the details I sent her. I love it," Elizabeth reiterated. "Thank you, Lindsey."

"No problem."

"I think we have everything sorted for your ceremony at the Lodge," Penny said. "I've booked you the gazebo near the pool and park area. It has a large circle drive and I was thinking you could arrive on the horse-drawn sleigh. What do you think?"

"Sounds heavenly," Elizabeth said. "Thank you so much for doing this for me. When you get married, I will plan yours."

Penny nodded but doubted she'd be getting married anytime soon. "That's not exactly in the cards for me."

"Why not? Will seems like a nice guy and he's not married already," Elizabeth said with a wink. "I asked."

"I did, too," Penny admitted. She quickly caught Lindsey up on her romantic track record with less-than-great guys.

"I've always been too busy to date and the only guys

I used to meet were competitors like me, and they all seemed too arrogant," Lindsey admitted. "But I do hope to get married someday."

Penny always had, too. But she had fallen for Will and he was not interested in marriage. By his own words, commitment wasn't for him.

"So what's the problem with Will?" Elizabeth asked after they changed back into their regular clothes and were having breakfast in her kitchen.

"He's not the marrying kind. He only does two-week relationships," Penny said.

"Uh, that's not what he told me," Elizabeth said offhandedly.

"What?"

"He's been married before," her friend explained. "We talked about brides and weddings when I ran into him in town."

A spark of anger started deep inside of her. All the excuses she'd been making for him...all the leeway she'd given him...now seemed like a big fat lie. Because the man who claimed he couldn't do anything longer than two weeks *could* do it. Just not with her.

WILL SAT IN the Lodge lobby listening to the Christmas music and watching the fire. He had a book in his hands. He preferred to read paperbacks over ebooks, though he did have the Kindle app on his iPad. But there was something about the tactile feel of the book in his hands that he liked.

He hadn't figured out what to do next with Penny, but he knew he could no longer deny that he wanted more with her. Now he just had to figure out how to bring it up. He had the thought that she might be amenable to meeting throughout the year for two weeks at a time until they figured out if this was a Christmas thing or something real.

Will rested his head against the back of the chair and closed his eyes. He thought he smelled Penny's vanilla-scented body lotion and turned to find her perched on the edge of the chair closest to him.

"Can we talk?" she asked.

He grinned. She looked so pretty she took his breath away. With her long silky hair, big blue eyes and those sensuous lips that always made him want to kiss her. He remembered the way she'd made love with him last night and knew he'd found something special with her. She was his equal on every level when it came to sex and her drive matched his. In fact, she complemented the things he was good at and evened out the things he'd never tried.

"Yes, of course. I wasn't sure when you'd be back from breakfast with your friends so I've been sort of hanging out and waiting for you. I wanted to speak to you, as well."

"That's good," she said, giving him a tight smile. "What did you want to discuss?"

"It's probably a conversation that would be better-suited to some privacy instead of here in the lobby," Will said. He hoped that when he suggested they continue their vacation affair, she'd be happy. But either way, discussing their private lives in the lobby didn't feel right to him.

"Sounds good. Want to go for a walk?" she asked. "There's a path that leads to a park. It's a location I need to check out again for Elizabeth's wedding."

"I'd like that. Let me get my coat from the coat check," he said. "I'll meet you back here in a few minutes."

She nodded. She still wore her coat and had the scarf he'd given her tied around her neck, but it felt like something was off. That he was missing something important. He claimed his coat and tucked the book into the pocket as he walked back to Penny.

He realized she hadn't touched him since she'd approached him. She always either hugged or kissed him whenever she saw him. He tried to pretend it wasn't important, but it felt as if it was.

Something had changed between last night and this morning. Perhaps he had been kidding himself when he thought that he could just keep things the way they'd always been. It had been wishful thinking to believe that he'd have what he wanted and still get her to agree to it.

He knew in business that risks had to be taken—but he was going to ask her to meet him again after Christmas. Wasn't that a big enough risk?

Perhaps she just didn't know where she stood with him. Maybe if he could convince her to give him more time…that would work.

He wasn't one to give in or give up lightly.

But as he headed back toward her, he stopped to observe her where she stood in the middle of the lobby by the fireplace. She looked small and lost, he thought with a pang. Unlike how he'd ever seen her before. He felt responsible.

He'd only wanted to give her a Christmas she wouldn't forget. Take the same thing for himself. But he seemed to have done something to hurt her. He wouldn't know what it was until they talked.

Will walked up to her, wrapping one arm around her,

and she gave him that stiff smile again as she pulled away. "Ready to go?"

"Not yet," he said gruffly. "What gives? Have I done something?"

She bit her lower lip. "I'd rather talk about that when we're alone."

"Fine. But I thought we left things in a pretty decent place when we went to sleep last night. I'm sorry I didn't hear you wake up this morning."

She shook her head. "It's not that. I was quiet so I wouldn't disturb you."

"Then what is it?" he asked, holding the door for her and she walked through, turning toward the path that led to the recreation area. He followed her. She was moving quickly. Her steps short and almost angry.

"Penny. We're alone here. Tell me," he insisted.

She stopped and shoved her hands into the pockets of her coat. Looked up at him with eyes that were sparking with outrage. "Tell me again how you always have two-week affairs because you can't commit to anyone longer than that."

"What?" he asked. "You know that's the truth. What's this about?"

"I had a very interesting conversation about weddings this morning with Elizabeth and was surprised to learn that you knew a little something on the subject of brides. That you'd been married."

*Oh, crap.* Kara was so long ago he didn't consider her anymore, but he understood how it might look to Penny.

"It's not what you think," he said.

"Really? Did you marry her?"

He felt cold deep inside his soul. This was not going to end well. "Yes."

"Then it's exactly what I thought," she said. "You're another liar."

# 15

PENNY SAW ON his face that he was scrambling to find an answer. Something to say that would placate her and make everything okay, but it was futile. She turned and stormed away from him and the Lodge. Walked farther down the snow-covered path and tried to force herself to remember he was only her two-week lover.

Forget that she'd started to believe he could be more. Forget that she had started to care about him and had hoped he cared about her, as well. Because Will had been playing her all along. Pretending to be one thing just so he could have his no-strings-attached affair.

The worst part was she would have been fine with it if he hadn't said he could *never* marry. She wouldn't have thought of marriage—she wasn't looking for forever. But knowing what he'd said, and the kind of closeness they'd shared since then, she felt betrayed.

She wanted it to just be anger. That would make it so much easier.

But it was hurt, too.

She'd been honest with him. Confided things that she usually kept carefully tucked away from the world to protect herself, but he'd made it seem as if it might be okay, and now she knew it wasn't.

He'd been playing a game. A different game than Butch had, but at the same time, it felt pretty damned similar.

"Penny!"

"Unless you have something new to say, something that will make up for the last week of you pretending that marriage was something you'd never consider, than forget it," she said.

He caught her arm and tugged her to a stop. "No."

"No?"

"That's what I said. I'm not going to let you throw out a comment like that and walk away." He spoke through gritted teeth, his eyes dark with pain. "The truth is, I was married when I was twenty-one. It lasted for less than a month and then it ended. I was horrible at being married and I learned from that and moved on. I never think of Kara as my wife, I think of her as a…mistake. I wished I'd been more mature so I wouldn't have made it."

She didn't want him to make sense. Didn't want to listen to him and let go of her anger. Part of her knew it was because if she were mad then she'd be able to just leave. Break things off with him now instead of letting her vulnerable heart become more attached to him.

Another part of her acknowledged it was too late.

"I'm listening."

"There's nothing more to tell."

"I think there is," she said. "Why didn't it work out?"

He sighed. "It's not a very flattering picture of me."

"That's okay. Your image isn't that great in my mind right now anyway."

He moved a few steps away from her and looked out at

the snowy landscape. "I had been alone for so long. First at boarding school and then at various summer camps and college. I dated Kara in college and we decided to marry. I never thought what it would be like when I had someone else to share my life."

She got it—he'd been alone. But she wasn't making the connections that would make this all seem sensible. He'd said he didn't do commitment, yet he had. That meant he'd lied. And she wasn't going to just let him off the hook. "What happened?"

He looked at her for a long moment. "I guess I panicked in a way. I got really possessive and didn't want her to leave my side. I had nightmares and woke up in a cold sweat. I scared her." He exhaled sharply. "She was willing to give me time to get over it, but I saw things in myself that I couldn't handle."

She felt a little sad when she thought of Will at that age. Finally finding someone to share his life and then being completely overwhelmed by it. "You were young."

"I was. I started drinking after she left and when I got sober, I realized that for me letting someone that close was like reopening the pain I felt when my parents left. I couldn't feel safe with Kara because I worried she'd die unexpectedly." There was a long pause. "So I stopped getting emotionally involved. I limited myself to two-week flings where there wasn't time to let anything serious develop." His jaw flexed as he stared into her eyes. "And that worked...until now."

Now? She didn't want to believe that she was different to him. But she could tell already she was. She had to believe that the love that had started growing in her heart would be mirrored in his.

"In what way?" she asked him.

"I can't just leave you on December 31," he said bluntly. "But I'm afraid to take a leap, as well. I wanted to ask you something, but first do you understand why I didn't mention my marriage?"

"Not really. I mean when you talked about how you were afraid of losing her, I get that. I think we all feel that way when we find someone to care about. I know I do."

"True enough, but it is so far back in my mind. That was fourteen years ago, Penny. I'm thirty-five and life looks a lot different now. I'm not the man I was at twenty-one, but those same demons still reside inside of me."

She looked at him with his thick head of light brown hair and intense blue eyes. That face that had become so dear to her over the last week…and she wanted to harden her heart. Find some way to keep herself safe from him. But she couldn't. "Is there anything else you haven't told me?"

"No."

"Think about it, Will. Be very sure before you answer. Because if I find out you've lied about anything else, I won't be able to forgive you," she said.

He closed the gap between them in two long strides, drew her into his arms and kissed her fiercely. "I promise you there is nothing else."

PENNY WALKED AROUND the gazebo and Will followed her. He really hadn't meant to talk about Kara with Penny's friend, but the truth was that Penny made him feel like his past wasn't a dark quagmire, and he was thinking about things that he hadn't really dwelled on in years. He trusted Elizabeth because Penny did…he had started to become involved with a community of people. She scraped some snow off the railing of the gazebo and turned to look at him.

"What do you think? I'm going to drape lighted garland around the pillars and the top. Pretty enough for a winter wedding?" she asked.

He shrugged. "You're asking me? Wedding planning isn't really my forte, but yeah, I guess it will be pretty enough. Is that what you want for your own wedding?"

"Wouldn't you like to know!" She curled the snow in her hand into a ball and he noticed it a second before she lifted her arm and lobbed the ball at him. He tried to duck but it caught him on the shoulder, splattering snow on his face.

"Oops," she said while laughing. "Sorry that hit you."

*Yeah, right.* "No problem."

Will noticed she was scraping more snow from the railings and he had a feeling he was about to become her target again. He reached down and grabbed a handful of snow, standing up just as another snowball hit him in the chest.

She giggled but when he looked up he couldn't see her. Then he noticed her pink knit cap behind one of the pillars of the gazebo.

He packed his snow into a round ball and strode toward her.

"Another misfire?" he goaded.

"Maybe," she said, popping out from behind the pillar to fire another snowball at him.

But he was ready this time and knocked hers away while throwing one of his own, which hit her on the shoulder. It shattered and got in her hair and on her hat.

She laughed and ran toward the open field behind the gazebo, and bent to scoop up another handful of snow.

He followed at a safe distance and made another snowball for himself. But as he bent to pick up more snow, he got hit on the back.

"Are there any rules to this game?" he asked in a mocking tone.

"Nope. I'm aiming to hit you when I can."

He fired one toward her and it hit her leg as she turned and ran toward the line of trees in the distance. He followed after her with his last snowball and tossed it as she turned to see where he was and it hit her square in the chest. She threw her arms out to the side and fell backward.

"You got me."

"I did," he said, walking over to her. She moved her arms and legs, making a snow angel, and he fell down a short distance from her and did the same.

"I'm sorry I didn't mention my marriage," he said as he moved his arms and legs. He'd never been with anyone he cared for as deeply as Penny, not even Kara. It scared him. Way more than he wanted to admit.

He looked over at her and noticed she was staring at him. "I just wanted to be special. Like the one woman who made you feel something more. And I thought I got you, but then when I learned about your marriage, I realized that I didn't. There are still things we haven't shared."

He sat up and turned toward her, messing up his snow angel. "I know. But you *are* special, Penny. Before you asked me about Kara, I wanted to talk to you about something that is important to me."

She nodded. "I'd get up but I don't want to ruin my angel."

He laughed and got to his feet. "Give me your hands."

She did and he lifted her straight up and caught her around the waist, setting her down next to her snow angel.

"Closest I'll get to wings," she said, wiggling her brows. Then she dusted the snow from her back and looked up at him. "What were you saying…?"

"Would you consider meeting me for vacations through the year? Giving the two of us a chance to see if there is more between us than just Christmas?"

Penny tipped her head to the side as she studied him. She licked her lips and then slowly nodded. "It will depend on my job situation. I'm going to be living off my savings until I get another position, but I would like that. I'm not ready to say goodbye to you yet, either."

He wrapped his hand around her gloved one, but she held him at her side, reaching up with her free hand to flick at the snow caught in his bangs. Then she kissed his jaw. "I'm not sure what to do with you, Will."

"I don't know how you mean?"

"It's hard because I've never gone into something like this knowing it will be just for fun."

"I know. You are making this all new to me. It feels like I've been waiting for you for my entire life and that scares me. Makes me want to retreat and yet, at the same time, I don't want to lose you." His Adam's apple bobbed up and down. "When I saw how angry you were earlier, I was afraid I wouldn't have any more time with you. I didn't want that."

"Why not?" she asked gently.

He couldn't confess to his emotions. Not now. Maybe not ever. He intended to do this until he had a chance to figure out how to keep Penny with him and not lose his mind in the process.

"It's not Christmas and I have some fun plans for us on that day."

She looked disappointed.

"I can't change overnight, Penny. I want more but I can't make any promises right now. I need to know that you're okay with taking this one step at a time."

PENNY FELT LIKE she'd been through the ringer today but there was something nice about standing in the snow with Will. Over his shoulder she saw their snow angels. Hers so perfect, thanks to him, and his just a little messier.

Sort of like the two of them. They were figuring things out together and his offer to see her again after the New Year was good. But already she knew it wouldn't be enough. She had to figure out what to do next. But not now.

She wanted to enjoy these next few days, and Christmas, and then she could try to deal with what would happen between them. She stepped back. "Want to go and bake some cookies with me?"

"No."

"Why? You have something else in mind?"

"Yes, in fact, I do. I want to go and make love to you," he said. "I want to make sure that everything is okay between us."

"Sex isn't an answer," she told him. "It didn't help last night, did it?"

"I thought it did," he said huskily.

"It left me feeling like I was grasping at you, trying to hold a man who was already gone."

He shook his head, then pulled her close, but she didn't want that. She realized that this was all like frosting on a cookie that had been broken. It might look nice on the surface but underneath the problems were still there.

And meeting for vacations was the same as what they had right now. In order for her to ever truly be happy with Will, she knew she was going to need more. Something that she feared he wouldn't be able to give her.

Learning about his marriage had revealed the truth that had been dancing just out of reach since they met. The solid reason why a handsome, successful man like Will was still a bachelor at thirty-five. And even though Penny was tempted to try to fix him—or change him—that wasn't going to happen.

Hadn't she learned anything from her mom and dad? It was like her mom said, love wasn't always hearts and flowers. Sometimes it hurt.

"What are you thinking?" he asked anxiously. "If it means that much, I'll make cookies with you."

She shook her head. There was no way she could explain this to him. She wanted to be the light, carefree girl she'd been when they'd met under the mistletoe, but she wasn't that same person anymore.

She would never be that girl again.

Falling for Will had changed something inside of her, and the way she'd fluttered through life, finding these meaningless little relationships that let her down, was no longer acceptable. She wanted it all.

"I can't do this," Penny said.

"Do what?"

"Pretend that I'm happy with a promise of more sexy vacations together. I think I want more from you," she admitted. "I'll understand if you don't. I get it. From what you said, that's not what you're looking for."

He dropped her hand. "It's not."

Blinking back tears, she nodded. It was the confirmation of what she'd already figured out for herself. "Okay. Then let's stick with our original arrangement."

"Are you sure? Seems like that isn't going to be enough for either of us," he said.

"What choice do we have? Spend the rest of our vacations in cabins next to each other, pretending we don't exist?" she asked. "That sounds ridiculous, doesn't it?"

"I don't want to do any of that. Why can't you agree to my suggestion?" He placed his hands on her shoulders and stared down at her intently. "It's a step forward."

"Because it's not really a solution. It's just postponing the inevitable. Unless you really do think you can change. Can you?" she asked softly. From everything he said and her own rotten luck when it came to men— Actually, that wasn't true. She didn't have rotten luck. She'd just spent so much time trying to keep from falling in love that it had snuck up on her when she wasn't looking.

And she wanted to believe that maybe that emotion was in his heart, as well. But the truth was, just because she had fallen for Will didn't mean he'd fallen for her. That wasn't the way the world worked.

There were no scales of fairness or balance that ensured couples loved each other equally. She knew that. So although she desperately wanted to cling to the hope that maybe things would be different, she knew she had to prepare herself for the worst.

Which meant steeling her heart and mentally readying herself to have this one and only Christmas with Will.

"So just our original agreement, then?" he asked.

"Yes. And sex is okay but no more spending the night together. That makes it feel like a relationship."

He hardened his jaw and shoved his hands in his pockets. Looking as if he wanted to argue but then thought better of it.

She sighed. The day that had started out so full of hope and promise was turning gray and stormy. Not just in her heart but also all around them. The snow clouds were heavy and the flurries started falling as they walked back toward the Lodge. A messenger from the concierge met them as they entered the lobby and told her that she had two packages waiting.

Will excused himself and told her he'd meet her later, and she watched him walk away. It hurt a little seeing him go, even though she knew she'd see him that evening. She told herself it was a view she should get used to, because before long he'd be walking away for good.

# 16

WILL WAS TEMPTED to go to the small grocery and sundries store in the Lodge and get a bottle of Glenlivet to take back to his room with him. He actually stopped in the store before he realized what he was doing. He couldn't let himself go backward, and yet at the same time he needed something to dull the pain he felt right now.

He hadn't wanted to hurt Penny or leave them both in this position, where there was no step forward and no way to go back.

He stood there in front of the whiskey display, trying to make himself leave, but he didn't want to. Sweet oblivion beckoned and all he had to do was reach out and pick up the bottle. He lifted his hand.

"Will?"

He glanced over his shoulder and saw Elizabeth standing at the end of the aisle. She gave him a tentative smile. He dropped his arm and walked over to where she was. Pretending he was okay. Faking it the best he could until he was alone. That was too damned close.

"Hi, Elizabeth."

"I think I might have spoken out of turn to Penny earlier," she began uncomfortably. "I didn't realize she wasn't aware of your marriage. I'm sorry."

He shook his head. "It's no problem. Besides, if you had known the circumstances beforehand, would you have really kept it from her?"

Elizabeth started to nod but then shook her head. "I couldn't. She's my best friend. I'd want to protect her if I could."

"I want to do the same. To be honest, it wasn't something I thought would matter," Will admitted. But he knew that Penny wouldn't like it if he discussed their relationship with her friend. "Thanks for being upfront with me."

"I felt I at least owed you a warning that I mentioned your marriage." Still looking uneasy, she cleared her throat. "So, how are you finding your stay at the Lodge?"

"Very nice."

Elizabeth nodded. "If there is anything I can do to make your stay more pleasant, please let me know."

"You've already gone above and beyond," he said. "I can see how the Lodge earned each of its five stars."

She flushed. "It's not really down to me. I've only been the GM for six weeks."

"Did you come in from another resort?" he asked, leading her away from the groceries and back out into the hallway. Now that he was talking, he started feeling normal again, like he didn't need the Glenlivet anymore.

"No, I have worked here for the last ten years. It's like a family. I doubt Lars would let an outsider have a position of power here or at his resort in the Caribbean."

"There aren't many resorts that can still have that kind of control over themselves," Will said.

"We're lucky that Lars has a great board who respect him. Most of them are friends he's made over the years. People who believe in his leadership and share his philosophy on running his luxury resorts," Elizabeth said. "I'd be happy to give you more information if you need it for your portfolio."

"Thank you," he said, but he had all the business information he needed from her. "I think I'm good for now."

"Okay, I will see you later." She flashed a smile. "Take care."

She walked away and Will made himself leave the store, as well. He headed toward his chalet but somehow ended up at Penny's instead. Taking a deep breath, he knocked on her door, and when she opened it, he stepped over the threshold.

"I'm sorry I can't be more."

"Don't be," she said. "We're going to have fun and pretend that each day is enough."

He wished it were that easy, but he was willing to give it a try because the alternative was that he headed back to the sundries store and bought that bottle of whiskey. She had two packages under her tree but not wrapped presents. They were big shipping boxes.

"What's in there?"

"Presents for you," she said with a half smile. "Are you someone who likes to peek?"

Will shook his head. Truth was, he hadn't received a present in years. He didn't have close friends and if he wanted something he'd get it for himself.

"I'm afraid I *am* the type that peeks," she confessed. "That's why my mom doesn't send my presents until the last minute. I wish I had your willpower."

"It's not willpower, I just don't get presents," he said.

"What? Why not?" she asked incredulously. She leaned back against the counter at the kitchen area, folding her arms across her voluptuous chest, studying him.

"I don't have friends or relationships that last more than two weeks. That makes it hard to have people who send you gifts," he said. It wasn't a topic he wanted to discuss, but he was curious as to what she might have gotten him. Two boxes, and they looked big. He'd already finished his shopping for her and thought she'd like the things he'd gotten her, but maybe he should get her a few more things…

"What about an assistant?" she asked. "My office-mates and I all exchange gifts with each other."

"I work alone at my home and do all my research myself. I do send a box of cigars to my attorney and all my clients get a gift from me, and they gift back, but it's corporate giving—chocolate or donations to charities."

He'd never thought about gifts before this. Well, at one point he had, but he'd stopped thinking about them long ago. To be frank, getting a present from someone who he didn't care about wasn't something he wanted or needed. But a present from Penny was something altogether different. *That* he wanted.

"I'm glad you have me this Christmas," she said tenderly. "That's what I decided when I was walking back here. We need each other."

"Yes, we do," he agreed. "And I'm very glad I have you to spend this holiday with."

WILL PUT SOME Christmas music on the television and then joined her in the kitchen. She had all the prepared ingredients—softened butter, eggs, sugar and flour—

ready to go into the bowl. Over the years she'd baked cookies with lots of people, but never with Will.

She thought of this as another gift she was giving him. Something he didn't know he was missing but years from now he'd remember fondly. "Do you want to do wet or dry?"

"Um...what?"

She smiled, guessing that his mind was elsewhere. "Ingredients. You have to combine them separately and then put them all together."

"Wet?" he asked.

"Okay, here you go—eggs, softened butter, vanilla and sugar," she said, handing him the measured items.

"Sugar is not wet," he said, frowning slightly.

"I know but you always have to cream the butter and sugar together first."

He read the recipe and was very serious about adding all the ingredients together while she sifted the flour and other dry ingredients together. "Feliz Navidad" started playing and she danced around the kitchen as the mixer was working at getting all the wet ingredients combined.

"When I was little I thought the words to this song were 'At least my name's Da.'"

He started laughing. "You're kidding."

"Nope. And I loved it—it was my favorite song so I used to sing it really loud whenever it came on the radio. One night my mom had some people from her work over for dinner and I was dancing around singing it and one of them said, 'What is she singing?'"

"Oh, no."

"Yes, and my mom replied, 'She just makes up the words,'" Penny said. "And I was like, 'No, those are the words, Mom.'"

She laughed at the memory and how funny it was to everyone. "After that my mom told me the correct lyrics but sometimes, just to tease her, I'll text her 'at least my name's Da.'"

Will put his arms around her and swayed with her to the music, singing softly in her ear, and she was surprised that he had such a nice voice. It was another little memory that she put in her heart to remember him by when he was gone. But she wasn't thinking about that, not today.

She looked into the bowl where he had been mixing away. "I think that's creamed enough."

"Okay. What now?"

She talked him through adding in the rest of his items and then slowly added hers in. "Now we have to roll it out. Where are your cookie cutters? The ones you bought the other day."

"In my chalet," he said. "I came straight here from the Lodge."

"I thought you had more time. We planned to bake the cookies tonight," she reminded him. "Didn't we?"

"I stopped at the sundries store and ran into Elizabeth," he said. "She wanted to warn me that she'd told you about my previous marriage. I guess she could tell by your reaction that I hadn't mentioned it. I told her it was not a big deal." He smiled at her. "She's a good friend to you."

"Really? How do you know?" Penny asked, but she already knew Elizabeth was a good friend. She just wanted to know why he thought so.

"She got a little protective toward you. I'm glad you have people like her in your life."

"Me, too," Penny said. "We've known each other a

long time. It helps when you share all the ups and downs, you know?"

He started to say something but she laughed before he could. "No, you don't."

"Maybe I will soon," he said gruffly.

"Really?"

"Yes, with you," he said, turning to grab his coat. "I'll go and get my cookie cutters."

"Okay, hurry," she said.

He lifted a brow. "Why? What's the rush?"

"It's just…I'll miss you while you are gone," she said. That was more than the truth. She had decided to enjoy the rest of her time with him, and after their conversation in the snow earlier, she didn't have any misconceptions that maybe it could be more. She knew this was it.

Will pulled her into his arms, tangled his hands in the back of her hair and kissed her. She loved the way his lips felt against hers. She breathed in his masculine scent and held him to her. A sentimental Christmas song was playing on the radio and she felt tears burning in her eyes as she thought about how this wasn't something that could last.

She wanted to tell him that she'd compromise and give up on her own pride just to keep him by her side. But she knew that would poison what she felt for him. And she didn't want to let that happen.

Will lifted his mouth from hers, stared into her eyes with that intense blue gaze of his and pulled her close. He rocked them back and forth to the music for several long, tantalizing moments before he spun out of her arms and strode to the door.

"I'll be right back," he said.

She swallowed hard and turned away, forcing herself

to stay busy mixing icing and coloring while he was gone. She pulled out the cookie cutters she'd bought when they were together but also the model train one she'd special ordered for him.

She set them on the counter and then washed the work surface, drying it before putting some flour down on it and getting out the rolling pin she'd purchased. She was going to have more baking supplies in her suitcase than she did at home, she thought ruefully.

She cut the dough in half and started rolling it out, getting it ready for Will when he got back. The smell of the cookie dough reminded her of all the batches of cookies she'd made over the years. All the memories she had of cookies baked and frosted and eaten in the kitchen. She wanted that with Will. Wanted him to have those special memories, as well.

WILL STOOD OUTSIDE in the cold, letting the weather cool him off. There were things he wanted that he never knew he'd longed for until he'd met Penny. And all of them were in that chalet. All of them centered around that one woman. He knew if he reached out and asked her to give him a chance, she'd do it.

But he also knew that in this moment he felt fear in his heart alongside all the deep emotion she stirred to life inside of him. It would be easy to pretend that he could handle it, but for the first time in almost ten years, he'd been tempted to drink.

Not just have a sip of something but to drink until he was numb and the world disappeared.

That was dangerous.

And when he held Penny in his arms, he wanted something so much more from her, wanted to never let her go. And he meant never. Not today or tomorrow or any of the days for the rest of their lives.

Not healthy.

He wondered if he should try to talk to someone. But who? His therapist had retired almost four years ago and he'd been doing so well. True, maybe it had been ego and cockiness that had made him believe that he could handle himself now that he was an adult. But he suddenly realized that he'd been fooling himself.

He hadn't understood it before because he'd been meeting women on his vacations that'd been happy to have something superficial and just for fun. Fun wasn't overrated. He worked hard and needed to blow off steam at these two-week holidays he scheduled. But this year he wasn't so much blowing off steam as turning into someone different.

The same thing that Penny had said she wanted, but *she* was different, too.

She had been from the first moment he'd kissed her under the mistletoe and he doubted that would ever change.

No distance or time was going to make him be able to handle this without coming up with a plan forward. He stood there for a few more moments. The snow that had been threatening earlier started to fall in earnest fat flakes. He ran to the porch of his chalet, let himself in and looked for the bag from the kitchen store.

There was so much that he was doing for the first time with Penny. Maybe that was why she felt so different than the other women he'd been involved with. Because she opened up his world and introduced him to new things.

He was baking and talking about childhood memories and having more sex than he had had in the last few years. She was a mix of sweet memories and sexy nights and he had no idea where to go from here.

He felt as trapped now as he had been as a lad of ten when his parents died. When he'd realized he had to figure out a way to keep going forward. He'd thought he'd figured it out long ago. But he hadn't been moving—he'd been standing still and hiding from life.

Penny made him want to be more. To be a better man. He knew he was a good man but he wanted to be one for her. Not just an investor with integrity. He wanted things that had nothing to do with business.

And as tempted as he was to experience more, to reach out and grab it with both hands, he was afraid, as well. The loss he'd suffered, he knew that he should have gotten over it by now and thought he had.

But it still haunted him.

He picked up the kitchen-store bag and left his little chalet. He was overthinking this. They'd already come to an arrangement and he needed to just keep to it, and when he got back to his home and his routine, everything would be fine.

Maybe if he said it often enough it would become the truth.

He knocked on her door and then opened it and walked in. She was standing there in the hallway with her coat on.

"What's up?" he asked, seeing she had her scarf in hand and her boots on, as well.

She chewed the corner of her lip and then took her coat off. "You were gone a long time and I was worried about you."

"I'm a mess, Penny," he blurted. "I don't know what

I'm going to do about you. I'm pretending that all I have to do is get through Christmas and then everything will be normal for me again, but I no longer believe that is true."

She looked stricken and he didn't want to be a burden to her or anyone.

"It's not you," he said, scrubbing a hand across his face. "It's just that my life had been a nice comfortable shade of brown before I met you, and now I've got all these colors all around me and I'm not sure what to do. I'm not sure if it's something I need to worry about or if it will all go away when I get home."

"I know exactly what you mean," she confessed. "I had those same doubts and worries when I learned you had been married but now I know that it's not anything I can control. I want to spend this time with you for the selfish reason that I want this memory to keep," she said.

"I'd like that, too," he said gruffly.

# 17

PENNY TOOK WILL'S hand and led him to the kitchen. She took out his cookie cutters and handed them to him. Inside she was dying a little, but on the outside she smiled and just carried on.

That was what she'd done when Butch's wife had surprised him in the office, very pregnant and very in love with her cheating husband. It was what she'd done when her father had shown up at her elementary school drunk and rambling. It was what she'd do now. She'd get through this and find some kind of Christmas joy—if it could be found.

"We aren't going to think about this anymore," she said. "I see you have some interesting cutters here."

She held up the robot.

Will didn't say anything and Penny turned away. He was shutting down again, for reasons she couldn't fathom, and she couldn't do this on her own. Not really. For her it came down to the fact that if he wouldn't at least try to be happy, she was going to have to…what? She didn't want to say goodbye. No matter how many times she tried to tell herself she was fine with it, she knew she wasn't.

And she wondered if there was really any sense in prolonging this for another day or even hour. She wanted the memories, but the pain she could live without.

"Good thing I have this big Santa-hat cutter," she continued in a voice that sounded way too chipper. "I'm making some cookies for the concierges, and thought I'd write their names on these in icing."

She took her cookie cutter and started cutting out the large Santa hats, and in a moment, Will came over next to her and took his robot and started using it. She'd set a parchment-lined tray on each side of the dough and one of the cookie spatula's she'd purchased.

Nat King Cole's "The Christmas Song" came on the radio and Penny couldn't help the tears that burned in the backs of her eyes. She missed her mom. She wished she were with the people who loved her and made her feel safe.

Having a sexy Christmas might have sounded good in theory, but the truth was that Will had changed that dynamic—or maybe she had by falling for him. She put her cookie cutter down and turned away from Will and the dough, braced her hands on the counter and tried to get her emotions under control.

"I'm sorry," Will said softly, coming up behind her and wrapping his arms around her.

She nodded. She didn't want him to see she was losing it. Just totally losing it while making cookies. That wasn't cool.

"Penny?"

"Mmm-hmm?"

"I really am sorry. I wanted to give you a great holiday but instead it seems like I have brought you down."

She turned to face him. "What has got me 'down' is the fact that you refuse to admit you aren't the same man you were at twenty-one. I'm not like your young bride. We could make a go of this."

"How do you figure?" he asked with a resigned sigh. "I know myself better than you do."

"You don't know yourself," she said. "You keep hiding in your safe world doing things the exact same way you always have. I think if you were honest, you'd have to admit that I'm different and that you picked me for this two-week affair because you were bored with your routine."

Will shoved his hands in his hair, watching her with those beautiful blue eyes of his, but right now his face was hard and almost angry. She got it. She hated having anyone point out her faults, but the truth was that he wasn't doing either of them any favors by acting like he knew for sure what he could or couldn't do. It had been fourteen years since he'd tried anything other than affairs.

And not that she was looking for marriage— All right, she wouldn't *mind* marriage to him. Because when he wasn't trapped in his past he was a great guy. He made her believe in the kind of happiness she'd always thought was just out of her grasp.

"I'm not bored," he said, through clenched teeth. "I'm just sure of myself and what I want. You are the one who seems to keep changing her mind."

"Really? Because I wasn't the one who took fifteen minutes to walk between our two places. I'm not the one who made it seem like cutting out a robot cookie was going to take all my willpower," she said, not holding back anything. She was tired of always falling for the wrong men. Giving them the goodness of her heart and all of her soul and finding them not worthy.

The worst part was, Will *was* totally worthy. She had seen the potential in him, and in them as a couple, over the intense days—and nights—they'd spent together. But instead of reaching out and taking what she had to offer, he was shoving her away.

Again she was being left alone. She was so tired of doing this.

"We're not all bubbly little Penny who can just smile and keep on going when things get tough." He crossed his arms over his chest. "Sorry if I'm not smiley enough for you."

She shook her head, feeling like he wasn't getting the point. Wasn't hearing what she was saying. Because she didn't need him to be smiling and happy. She just needed him to at least try.

"Will, smiles aren't what I'm asking for. And I know I use that happiness as a defense mechanism sometimes… but it's my way of not breaking down and totally losing it," she said. "All I want from you is to try. To meet me halfway."

"I thought I had by saying we could plan to meet up again in the spring or summer," he muttered in frustration. "That's more than I've offered anyone else before."

She looked at him. "Seriously? That's the exact same thing we have now. How is going on vacation again together going to be moving forward? We'd still be two people who haven't done anything but get together in a stress-free environment and have great sex."

"So?"

This wasn't working. No matter what he said to the contrary, he didn't want to change. Didn't want to take a risk on…what? Did he love her? Did he care about her? Or was this about something else entirely? "Will, what is it that you are so afraid of?"

WHAT *WAS* HE AFRAID OF? Before all this, he'd have said nothing. He lived his life on his own terms. But this last week with Penny had proven that he did still have a few spots in his dark soul that were driven by fear. She had exposed them, shed light on them, and now she wanted him to talk about them.

Not happening.

He'd wanted sex and fun for Christmas. Had that been too much to ask? Why couldn't she just keep smiling… except she had been, and he'd seen straight through her pretend smiles to the aching hurt underneath.

Hurt he knew he'd caused.

He was mad. At himself. At his parents for dying and leaving him a big mess, which he'd thought he'd gotten over, but part of what she'd said was right. He'd ignored it, buried it deep inside of himself, and then hunkered down in his routine to move on.

And most of all, he was mad at her. For reminding him of all the things he had missed. But he couldn't tell her that. Instead, he clenched his hands into fists, standing with his legs braced apart, as he looked her square in the eye.

"I'm not afraid," he said. He'd given her too much already and that was part of the problem.

She'd made him feel from the first moment they'd met that he could let his guard down, and that had been a huge mistake. One he wasn't going to repeat.

"Liar. I thought we said no lies, and now every time we talk, I'm hearing more and more untruths from you," she told him. "But you know what? That's not the worst part. You know you're lying to yourself, as well. That's where the real destruction will be. I think you probably buy into your own lies."

"What about you? Smiling when you know that you're not happy inside is a lie. But you think that's okay. There's a big double standard here, Penny. One that works in your mind and operates in your favor alone." He flattened his lips, growing angrier by the moment. "I offered you something more. Something that I've never even considered with anyone else, but that's not good enough for you, is it?" This wasn't entirely his fault. She was stuck in her routine as much as he was his. "You're so used to being treated poorly by every man that you automatically go into that mode if things aren't perfect. I haven't treated you badly. I'm not some loser who wants to hide you from the world."

"That's not fair," she said.

"It's not, but it is true. That truth you are supposedly so fond of. It hurts, doesn't it? To find out that you're not the one who's right all the time. That maybe you don't know it all."

"I never said I knew it all. I'm just saying—"

He scowled at her. "That you want everything your way. All the cards stacked in your favor. You want me to be the one to take all the risks. I'm not going to do it," he said at last.

"I guess that's all I need to know. I thought we had something special," she choked out.

"I'm not saying we didn't. But if it's so special to you, why can't you try doing things my way?" he asked.

He wanted to hang on to his anger, but the truth was, as she stood there looking so small and vulnerable, he wanted to say the hell with it and do whatever he had to in order to make this right. But then he remembered the bottle of Glenlivet and how close he'd come to buying it. He knew that in order to keep himself under the tight control he'd always had, he wasn't going to be able to do this any way but his.

"I can't," she whispered. "I know you think I'm just being petulant, but the fact of the matter is, I have waited a long time to find a man like you, Will. Someone who checks all the boxes in my head and in my heart. Some of those boxes I didn't even know were there, so pretending that it doesn't matter is not something I can do."

She walked over to him and put her hand on his arm, squeezed his bicep and then let her hand drop. "I want it all with you because I know if we tried, if both of us stopped living in fear, we could make it work."

But deep down, Will thought, she didn't know that. After all, how could she? Penny had no more experience with making a relationship work than he did. "How can you be so certain? Neither of us has ever been in this situation before."

"I realize that," she said, taking a step back. "But at least I'm willing to try."

"Don't say I'm a coward again, Penny. You have no idea of the battles that I have to fight every day."

She bit her lower lip and stared at him through a sheen of tears. "You're right—I don't. I'm sorry for your struggles and I don't want to make them worse. But I can't just stand here and let you push me away time and again and keep making excuses for you."

"I'm not asking you to. Why is meeting again later

next year not good enough for you?" he asked. "That's a big thing. Like I mentioned before, we'd have a chance to see each other again and we'd know if what we feel now is real."

She shrugged. "But we wouldn't. Real is give me your phone number at home and tell me where you live so we can figure out how to see each other as soon as we get back. But you don't want to know where I live. You don't want to see my real life."

She had a point. Real life was harder than vacations, harder than making this two weeks work. And he knew he wasn't sure he could do it.

"I can't."

PENNY WASN'T SURPRISED. She'd seen it in the way he'd been acting since they'd met up in the Lodge this afternoon. Also, despite what she'd told him, a part of her really didn't believe in her own feelings. She'd spent most of her life running from love, and having found it now, she wondered if she'd ever be able to enjoy it.

"I guess you can leave, then," she said tightly. No sense in prolonging the inevitable now that he'd made up his mind. Plus, he'd said some mean things to her.

"Fine. But before I do, I want to make sure you know that I didn't want to walk out on you. I didn't start this with the intent to deceive you—"

"I know that, Will. God, we both had the best intentions, but the truth of the matter is that we weren't in the right place to meet. Maybe a few years from now, when I've gotten used to my new life, I'll be better. But right now I think I was searching for some kind of happy ending in my life. If not with my job, then at least with you."

"Just a happy ending?" he asked. "Then I don't matter? Any guy would have done?"

"Not at all," she said vehemently. "*You're* the reason I want more. The reason why I started to believe that love could be more than the lousy examples I've seen. You're not a cheater or a drunk."

She looked at him and this time she didn't feel as angry as she had before. She felt sad for herself, and for him, because in her mind she thought if they could have both bent a little in their beliefs they might have been able to figure out a way to make this last.

"I almost wish I wasn't so stubborn," he ground out. "But I am. And I know what can happen if I don't keep myself under control. I'd hate myself if I hurt you, Penny."

She nodded. She'd already figured that out. If she were different, if her romantic past had just once had something positive in it, maybe she would keep dating him from vacation to vacation…but she knew better. She knew that half measures were the biggest lie she could tell herself.

And with Will she needed more.

"Nah, if you weren't stubborn, I wouldn't have grown to care so deeply for you," she said. Penny couldn't bring herself to call it love. Not right now when she felt raw and ached inside. She wanted to keep a part of her pride and not let him see how hard this was.

"I guess that's something," he said. The anger had cooled in him, as well.

Penny walked past him, but he caught her wrist, wrapped his arms around her and pulled her close for a hug. She turned her head to the side as the scent of his aftershave surrounded her, and she tried to remember that this was going nowhere, but when he tightened his arms, she wanted to say to hell with it.

She wanted to just pretend that she didn't care if she ended up brokenhearted and alone. But then she knew that was a lie. No more lies, she reminded herself.

She rose on tiptoe and kissed the beard stubble on his jaw then stepped back away from him.

He drew her back into his arms and brought his mouth down on hers. It was tender but she could feel the tension in him, the residue of anger beneath the surface. She met his passion with her own, and they held each other until the fire burning between them was extinguished.

"Thank you for a really enjoyable time," she said. "I hope that you find what you are looking for two weeks at a time."

He stared down at her, his blue eyes smoldering with emotion once again. "Why is meeting again later this year such a bad idea to you?"

She finally realized that until he knew the truth of how she felt, he was going to think she was simply trying to manipulate him. She tucked a strand of her hair behind her ear and tipped her head to the side.

Taking a deep breath, she said, "Because I love you, Will. I've never let myself love another man before and I'm not asking for anything back from you. I know that love isn't something that can be weighed and measured and sometimes one person falls and the other one doesn't."

He started to speak, but she held her hand up.

"If I met you for a vacation, I'd spend every minute we were apart making you into the kind of man who would love me. The kind of man who had missed me so much that when we met up again, I'd be anticipating that you felt the same way as I did. But that's not going to happen." She sighed. "And then, when I came to terms with that, I'd convince myself that I could do two weeks because two weeks is better than nothing, but in the end I'd be dying inside."

He didn't say anything, just shook his head. "I don't know what to say. I care so deeply for you, Penny. You've shaken me to my moorings. But that leap to where you are standing, that place where you look and see a happy future, I'm not sure I can do it."

She knew that. She'd sensed it from the moment he'd returned with his cookie cutter and stood next to her as if he were afraid of what might happen next. Will's life hadn't been the blend of happy days mixed with sad ones that hers had.

"I know. That's why I think this is goodbye," she said brokenly.

She wished he'd left when they'd been arguing because then she'd have the hope that it had been anger driving him away. This quietness as he walked to the door was a million times worse. Because this was really goodbye.

He was leaving for good and all she could do was watch him go.

# 18

CHRISTMAS EVE DAWNED crisp and cold. Penny rolled over and hugged the pillow that Will had slept on when he'd spent the night with her. Last night had been long, with lots of Ben & Jerry's and tons of tears, but she'd made it. Each day would be easier.

She didn't have to worry about texts from Will. She knew that the break with him was clean and forever. He wasn't going to send her messages, begging her to change her mind, which made her sad because for him she thought she might change. But she knew that was just loneliness talking. She respected herself too much to settle for half measures. Penny forced herself to get out of bed even though a part of her wanted to turn on the television and mope around all day. Surely she could give herself permission to do that for one day, but she suspected that would make tomorrow even harder for her.

Her mom wasn't here, her friends would be spending Christmas with their loved ones and she, who had said she wanted to be alone this year, was going to get exactly what she'd claimed she wanted.

A big lonely day.

She went and had a hot shower, trying to ignore the bathtub and the memories she had of Will washing her hair and pretty much making her fall for him. He'd done things for her that no other man had before. Things she hadn't even thought would be sexy or romantic, but they had been.

She got dressed and then checked her phone. As if he'd send a message…and what was she hoping for? He wasn't going to suddenly realize he loved her and run back to her. But it would be so perfect if he did.

Shaking her head, she gathered the box of cookies she'd made for the front desk and concierge staff and left her chalet, defiantly not looking toward Will's place. The snow from last night sparkled in the morning sun, and Penny stopped thinking about heartbreak and loneliness and tipped her head back. God, it was a pretty day.

The kind of day that made her happy to be alive. She felt tears burning her eyes but that was just because she'd realized that she would be able to put one foot in front of the other. Once more, she'd be moving forward on her own and somehow, some way, she had to make that okay.

She entered the Lodge and the bellman greeted her by name and smiled as she walked by. There were worse places to recover from a broken heart, she thought. And to be honest, if falling for Will had shown her one thing, it was how superficial her feelings for Butch had been.

She hadn't realized what love felt like until Will had taken her on that sleigh ride and she'd seen her first glimpse behind the facade of that sexy smile and charming wit.

"Good morning, Ms. Devlin," Paul, the concierge manager, said as she walked up to his desk.

"Morning, Paul. I baked these for your staff to say

thank you for all the help you've provided with Elizabeth's wedding arrangements."

"It was our pleasure," he said. "Do you need anything else to prepare for Christmas?"

She needed something that he couldn't procure for her. Even though the concierges here at the Lars Usten Lodge were incredible, there were some miracles they couldn't perform. She smiled at him and shook her head, then walked down the hall toward the model village. Suddenly, tears blurred her eyes again as she remembered how Will had looked when he'd seen the train.

That special smile on his face, the one she'd seen on only one other occasion. After they'd made love the first time. He'd been truly happy when he'd recalled his childhood memories. Why was he resisting being happy with her forever? Why didn't he have the guts to risk his heart?

She did.

But while she was used to having relationships, Will had confessed that he wasn't. That he liked to keep himself all tucked safely away so that he wouldn't be tempted down the dark path of addiction. But was that the truth?

Or was it really just the fact that she wasn't the kind of woman he wanted to have in his life for more than a few weeks? Of course she didn't want to believe that. It would be too painful, and much too personal. Instead, she wanted to make some sort of blanket excuse that would seem like it was his failing, and not hers, that had driven them apart.

But like love, it wasn't all one-sided. She knew she was just as much at fault for needing and wanting more. She hadn't wanted to change him and didn't want to admit he had already changed her. But at the end of the day, she was looking for more from Will than she'd ever allowed herself to dream was possible before.

She sat on the bench and watched the train chug around the little village, and thought of the gift she'd bought for him. The one that was in a box in her chalet. She knew that no matter what, she still wanted him to have it.

Even if he couldn't be her man and didn't love her, he deserved to have a Christmas memory that he could cherish. Something to hold on to for the rest of his life.

Penny got up and walked slowly back toward the lobby, and when she heard the Christmas music playing, she couldn't imagine the thought of spending Christmas Eve alone instead of with Will in her arms. Despite the problems they still faced, she knew that the one thing she really wanted this Christmas was to see him standing outside her door. A part of her was disappointed when she walked back to her chalet and he was nowhere to be seen.

Nevertheless, she wrapped the presents she'd bought for Will and arranged for the concierge to have them delivered to him tonight while she was at the community nativity play. She wanted to make sure he didn't think she'd sent them so he'd come and find her. On the contrary, she simply wanted to do this one last gesture for him. The man who'd shown her what it was like to be in love.

PARK CITY WAS decked out in lights, and Penny tried not to feel that tug of nostalgia as she walked into the church for their children's mass and evening nativity service. But she did. She remembered all the masses she'd attended with her mom as a child. How, as she'd gotten older, they'd exclaimed over the cute kiddos in their costumes, and how her mom had said someday Penny would be a mom.

She knew it was foolish to let herself get too depressed about that. Because deep down she knew she'd find a man and have kids, if that was what she wanted, but tonight she couldn't help thinking about the kids she'd never have. A little boy with Will's dark hair and her smile, and maybe a sweet girl with Will's bright blue eyes and her hair.

"Is this seat taken?"

She glanced up to see Lindsey standing there. "No, it's not. I thought you had plans."

"I did, but they fell through. My friends are still on the competitive team so they couldn't take the day off as they'd hoped."

"I'm sorry."

"It's okay," Lindsey said. "I've actually been enjoying scouting out Park City. I've been living here since the summer but haven't really spent that much time in town."

"Why not?"

Lindsey shrugged. "I think I was still in training mode. I pretty much stay at the Lodge and just ski and teach skiing and then go back to my condo." She gave a little laugh. "Boring, huh?"

Penny smiled at the other woman. "It's hard to change your routine."

In a way, Lindsey was like Will. Stuck in her life, and even though her circumstances had changed, she still hadn't moved forward. Penny hoped that Lindsey wasn't stuck in that routine forever. "Park City is nice. Do you see yourself staying here for a while?"

"I don't know. I'm hoping to give competing another

try once this knee is completely healed. My doctor wants me to give it another couple months but I feel so much stronger now, and it's been almost a year since the accident and my surgery."

Penny understood what it was like to be in limbo and ready to get back on track. That was sort of how she felt about her career and the fashion house that had promised her they'd get back to her in January. "I hope you can."

"Me, too," Lindsey said. "But if not, I'll find something else to do. I have had a few offers from a television station to do their winter sports commentary. I might give that a shot."

"Maybe you'll get famous and I can say I knew you way back when," Penny said with a laugh.

"Who knows?" Lindsey replied. "In any event, I was glad to see a familiar face tonight. I love nativity plays."

"Same here. I used to think I was the star every year when my mom would drive me to church dressed in my peasant costume. Though one year I did get to be the angel."

"With your long blond hair, my preacher would have made you an angel every year."

"You're blonde, too," Penny pointed out. "Were you an angel?"

"Nah, I started training when I was eight so I didn't have time for plays and all that. But my little sister did."

"You sound envious."

"I guess I sort of was. Sounds surprising, right? I mean, I really loved skiing and everyone put me first. My parents had to sell one of their cars and my dad worked two jobs so my mom could drive me to my private lessons, so I get how much they sacrificed for me.

But there were times when I wanted to be a normal girl, you know?"

Penny understood that. She'd loved her mom and had had a wonderful upbringing, but there had been times when she'd wanted to be like everyone else. Have a family with a mom and a dad, maybe a sibling or two. But the older she got, the more she realized that no one had an ideal childhood. Hers was so much better than a lot of others, especially Will's.

The play started with the kids walking up the aisle like the procession to Bethlehem. Penny sat back on the hardwood bench and got swept away, forgetting all the troubles that had been plaguing her since Will had walked out last night.

When it was over, Lindsey saw some fellow ski instructors and went to join them. She'd invited Penny along but she didn't want to go and have to act like she was happy tonight. Instead, she strolled down the main street of Park City, looking at the Christmas displays in the windows, and then, when she was sure her presents would have been delivered to Will and enough time had passed that he wouldn't come looking for her, she caught the shuttle van back to the Lodge.

There was a darling family on the same shuttle. The kids were talking excitedly about Santa and they kept gazing out the window at the stars and the night sky, searching for his sleigh being pulled by Rudolph and his red nose.

She remembered her night ride with Will and knew that was the moment she'd started to fall in love with him. Under the stars, talking about following Fido and those dreams from her childhood that had turned into different desires as an adult. She missed him.

She admitted that to herself as she walked into the Lodge and grabbed herself a bottle of wine and another pint of Ben & Jerry's ice cream from the sundries shop. She wished there was a way to take his past and hers away from both of them so they could be the perfect partners for each other. But she knew that wouldn't happen.

It had started snowing as she walked back to her little chalet and she looked up at the night sky, searching for something but knowing it couldn't be found.

WILL'S DAY HAD been spent on the phone trying to secure a job for Penny. He didn't want to just leave her without giving her that. One of his friends who owned a winery in Napa Valley was in desperate need of an event planner and was willing to talk to her. He made a note of it and neatly printed out all of the information for her, and had it sent to her room.

Then he decided he'd had enough of relaxing and he was ready to go home. He tried to change his flight but December 24 was a busy travel day, something he normally would have been aware of, but because he'd been so consumed with thoughts of Penny, he hadn't paid close enough attention. He was able to change his flight to December 27, but that was still three long days away.

He wasn't sure he was strong enough to stay away from her. But for the sake of his sobriety, he knew that he had to. After he'd left her chalet yesterday, he'd gone to the sundries store, bought the Glenlivet, and now that bottle sat on the counter in his kitchen. It was unopened so far, but every second that he wasn't working on his computer, he glanced over at it.

It promised the kind of relief from the pressure inside of him that nothing else could offer.

Finally after lunch, when he'd almost cracked the seal on the bottle, he left the chalet and went for a walk. Being outside helped because it was bitterly cold and left no time to think about what could be. Instead, he just concentrated on putting one foot in front of the other, following each breath as it puffed out in front of him.

He wanted Penny to give in and say that she'd be his vacation lover for the rest of his stay here, but he knew that wasn't going to happen. She wasn't going to just give up on what she wanted.

The thing was, he almost believed if she'd just say yes this one time, that he'd change. That wasn't realistic but she made him want to. Penny was unique and no matter how much he'd tried to make her like every other woman, that had never happened.

She'd thrown her phone out her door and almost cracked him in the head. God, she was wonderful. She was exactly what he'd needed for too long but he was afraid for himself. That was it. The truth he'd been running from for too long.

She made him want to be the man she needed because he sensed she could be the one person that he'd been searching for since he was ten years old and all alone. Penny got him, even the dark parts, and she made him better.

But at the same time…if he hurt her, if she got hurt, he wasn't sure he could deal with it.

He ran, trying to distance himself from the frenzied images in his head, left the path and found himself under the trees and sheltered from the view of anyone who might be walking by. He fell to his knees and, putting his head in his hands, let the quiet of the day fall around him.

He finally admitted to himself that he couldn't live

without Penny. He had known that for a while, and even though being with her might be a challenge, anything would be better than this aching loneliness.

It had only been one day and already he wanted to share things with her. He wanted to have her next to him as he'd planned for the New Year. And not for only two weeks. For much, much longer. But he couldn't go back to her.

He missed the feel of her in his arms, her sweet, feminine scent surrounding him.

Not now. He had to figure himself out first. What did the future look like?

She'd said she loved him and he'd walked away because that was easier than admitting that he felt more for Penny than he had for any other being in his life. He loved his parents, he knew that, but the feeling had been gone for so long—*they'd* been gone for so long—that he had forgotten what that had felt like.

And his marriage had been a mess of two needy people trying to make something real out of nothing. But he and Penny had found that, for them, nothing had turned into something very real.

He got up, realizing the snow had soaked through the knees of his jeans, but the cold numbness didn't bother him. It was stinging as he walked back to his chalet. Reminded him he was alive and that life wasn't ever meant to be easy or perfect.

Finally, he felt like he understood why he had been so unsure of what to do with Penny. Why he'd been unable to resist her for so long. She had found her way into his heart without him even being aware of it. He'd been charmed by her. Enchanted by her. And he'd been afraid to admit that he loved her.

That he needed her in his life for the rest of it.

He knew he'd be a mess if she was ever taken from him, but he would learn to handle that. Each day she made him stronger.

He entered his chalet and the first thing he did was throw the bottle of Glenlivet in the trashcan. Then he changed his clothes and got down to the business of figuring out how to win back the only woman he'd ever loved.

# 19

Will took a shower and got dressed in the Santa suit that the concierge had special ordered for him. It had taken them the better part of the day to get it for him, but he didn't mind. He had what he needed now to make this the best Christmas ever.

There was a knock on his door and he went to open it. One of the hotel staff had a trolley with wrapped presents on it.

"Hello, Mr. Spalding."

"Merry Christmas," Will said.

"To you, too, sir. These are for you. Where would you like them?"

Will stepped back into the hallway. "Under the tree, please."

It had been years since he'd had any presents and he knew these had come from Penny. That despite what had been said between them yesterday during that heated argument, she'd still sent him the presents she'd bought for him. It made him feel humble but also more in love with her than ever. If he needed the confirmation that she was his other half, the part that would make him a better man, well, then this was it.

He tipped the bellboy as he left and then went to sit under the tree and look at the packages. One of them was bigger than the others but he truly had no idea what was in any of them. She wasn't planning to see him open the gifts…that much was clear.

Had he waited too long to go to her? He didn't care. He seldom lost when he put his mind to something, and he definitely had put his mind to Penny.

He sat on the floor in front of the presents and reached for the big one. He felt like he had when he'd been a boy and saw the presents under the tree that he and his parents had decorated. That anticipation laced with joy in the pit of his stomach. Not all that different from how he felt when he thought about Penny.

Will pulled the package toward him, slowly removed the wrapping and then felt shock reverberate through him as he realized she'd gotten him a model train. The same one that he'd admired in the lobby of the Lodge. The one he'd said he and his father had been working on together.

He sat the box on his lap and just looked at it. Realized that his hands were shaking. Penny had given him something he wouldn't have bought for himself because he wouldn't have wanted to admit how much he wanted it.

He opened the box and set the train up in the living room, taking his time with the track, and it felt almost like his father was there with him, watching him. For the first time that he could remember, he was thinking of his parents and it wasn't about the loss of them. It was about what they had both given him.

He set the train on the track and then sat back on his

heels and flicked the button so that it fired up and started chugging around the living room.

He left the train on as he opened the other presents she'd given him. There was a wool sweater with his initials monogramed on it. And then a pair of socks that had the three wise men on camels following the Star of Bethlehem. But it was the smallish flat package that he opened last. The one that held the picture of the two of them that he'd taken when they'd been kissing that really got to him.

He'd thought nothing could top the train but this did. She was the gift that he hadn't known he wanted. The one thing that he truly needed. He remembered every detail of that day. How her lips felt under his. The way she'd felt tucked up against his side, and how in that moment he'd realized how much he was starting to care for her.

He'd been a little scared but still so sure that he'd be able to manage that fear. And he felt that way again. He'd been running for a long time but it was only when he turned his back on Penny that he knew he had to stop.

There was no peace or happiness down the path of his life if he was by himself. Nothing was worth it without her by his side.

He thought of the gifts he'd gotten her, superficial things that he'd sent to lovers over the years, and he realized that he needed to do something for Penny that would show her how much she meant to him. Jewelry was nice but he wanted something that would be about the two of them.

He wanted to do more.

He glanced at his watch. It was six-thirty on Christmas Eve and he wanted to go and find a present. Talk about awful timing. But that wasn't about to stop him.

He changed out of the Santa suit and into a pair of jeans and the sweater that Penny had gotten him and left the chalet. He walked quickly through the snow-covered path toward the Lodge, and when he got there, he waited until the concierge manager, Paul, was free.

Then he cornered him and asked for a very special favor.

Paul wasn't too certain he could pull it off, but then he'd been working at the Lodge for a long time so he had the contacts that Will needed. He rented an SUV while Paul got him the information and then he left with a name, a number and directions that led him out of Park City to a rural farmhouse.

And after two cups of coffee—and promises that he was a decent man who would give it a good home—he left the farmhouse with a rescue corgi named Fifi. He knew that Penny wouldn't be expecting it. And to be honest, as Fifi whined in her crate as he drove back to the Lodge, he knew he hadn't been expecting her, either.

PENNY LIT A fire in the chalet, texted her mother Merry Christmas so she'd be the first one to message her on Christmas morning, and then changed into her pajamas and wrapped the scarf that Will had given her around her neck. Sighing wistfully, she sat down on the couch next to the tree, looking at the presents underneath it from Lindsey and Elizabeth and Bradley. It was nice that she was close to her friends. They'd invited her to join them for dinner tomorrow.

She had not taken them up on it and if she hadn't agreed to plan out Elizabeth and Bradley's wedding, she'd be tempted to leave Park City altogether. But she had and her best friend needed her.

She'd gotten the small note card from Will with the information for a job interview from a winery in California. Even though it hadn't been what she'd really wanted from him, she was grateful all the same. It was another avenue for her to pursue, and she'd never lived on the West Coast. Still, deep down, she didn't know if she could really relocate there.

She was too used to being close to DC and all that. She wondered if Will was from California. Then laughed. Why did she care? It was pretty obvious that he'd broken all ties with her. That the job interview was his way of making amends for hurting her feelings and letting her move on.

She wished it were that easy. She took a sip of the hot chocolate she'd made for herself and listened to the logs in the fire and the clock ticking on the wall. She was staying out of her bed, not because she thought that Santa might appear but because she just couldn't spend another night on the bed she'd shared with Will.

Memories of him were everywhere in the chalet. She thought she'd ask to move to one of the rooms up in the Lodge but then changed her mind. She liked being surrounded by him for as long as she could.

She was pitiful, she told herself. But then again, she was in love. Though, at this moment, it was hard to see the difference.

She heard a knock on her door around 11:00 p.m. and padded over to it and looked out the peephole. There stood a bellman with a pile of presents. Unless she was wrong, they were from her mom.

She opened the door and pasted a bright smile on her face. "Merry Christmas!"

"Merry Christmas," the young man replied. "I had

orders to wait until midnight to deliver these, but my girlfriend got off early and…"

"It's okay, your secret is safe with me. Can you put them under the tree?"

"I did the same thing for your neighbor about five hours ago."

He must have delivered her gifts to Will. "Did he seem to like them?" she asked.

"He seemed surprised to me," the bellman said as he finished arranging the wrapped presents under the tree.

Penny got some cash for a tip for him from her wallet and then handed it to him as he walked out the door. "Thank you. Have fun with your girlfriend."

"I hope to. I'm planning to ask her to marry me. Got to plan it the right way, though," he said.

"I bet. Good luck…I hope she says yes."

"Thank you, ma'am."

Penny closed the door as the bellman walked away. She thought of the nervousness mingled with the joy on his handsome young face. She hoped he got his Christmas wish.

With a heavy heart, she walked over to the tree and looked at the presents there. She sat down next to them and admitted to herself that she'd trade all the presents for one more day with Will. Maybe she should just take him up on his offer of a string of vacation affairs.

Was that offer still on the table? She wasn't too sure. That note with the job offer seemed like his final communication with her. Maybe it was time for her to…pour herself a glass of wine and start opening presents. Penny went into her kitchen and uncorked the bottle of white wine and then went back to the tree. She knew she should wait until midnight to open her mom's gifts. But it was technically only five more minutes until Christmas, so maybe if she opened the presents from her friends first, she'd be able to make it till then.

So she sat cross-legged on the floor and set her wineglass on the coffee table. Feeling an unexpected wave of childlike excitement, she pulled Lindsey's beautifully wrapped present toward her and carefully opened the package. It was a long narrow box, and when she opened it up, she found a pair of cashmere-lined leather gloves in a deep pink color that she loved. She slipped them on and then, because she was by herself, took a picture of the gloves and popped it on Instagram, tagging Lindsey in it.

She took the gloves off and placed them back in the box with the lid off. It was something her mom always did. So that for the rest of Christmas Day when they looked under the tree they could see all the presents lined up and on display.

Next she opened the present from Bradley and Elizabeth. It was a heavy, large square box. Inside she found a new pair of snow boots in her size and a matching pair of leggings and a sweater. All from Fresh Sno, which was the chain of outdoor retail shops that Bradley owned.

She arranged them in the box and tried for an arty photo for Instagram. Then, disgusted with herself, she tossed her phone aside. Making believe she was having a great Christmas by posting stuff on social media was totally lame.

She didn't want to spend the holiday alone. Decision made, she stood up and put on her new snow boots and her gloves. She was going to find Will. No more pretending she was okay with being apart from him.

She'd convince him that they should be together this Christmas morning and every other morning that was yet to come. The doorbell rang and she opened the door… hoping for Will…but found a dog on her step with a big red bow around its neck. A note tied to it read "My name is Fifi and I am so glad I finally found you."

She bent down to pet Fifi—a cute little tri-colored corgi—and the pooch licked her hand. She glanced up and down the path but couldn't find anyone. She brought the dog inside wondering if this gift was from her mom. She got a bowl in the kitchen and put some water in it. The little dog wagged her tail and lapped at the water.

There was a loud knock on the door that startled her. Fifi started barking and ran to the door.

"Ho! Ho! Ho!"

The deep voice sounded like Santa, and when she looked through the peephole, she saw Will in a Santa suit standing on her doorstep.

She opened the door.

"Merry Christmas, Santa," she said.

Fifi leaped forward and wagged her tail as she tangled herself around his legs.

"Merry Christmas, Penny. I see Fifi finally found her way to you," Will said in a deeper-than-normal voice.

"Yes, she did. Thank you."

"You're welcome. Um…can I come in?" he asked in his normal voice. "I have this all planned out."

"Why do you want to come in?" she asked. Even though she wanted to throw her arms around him, she suddenly felt a bit gun shy. Unsure of his true intentions.

"Penny, you said you loved me and I was a fool to not tell you in that moment how I felt about you."

She swallowed and took a step back, gesturing for him to come inside. He did and closed the door behind him.

"First things first," he said, reaching into the big red

sack he carried. He took out two dog bowls and handed them to her along with a can of dog food. "She couldn't carry her own food. So I figured I'd bring it for her."

"Thank you," she said. "Why don't you go into the living room while I feed Fifi?"

"I will."

"Thank you for getting me this dog. I love her already," Penny said. And she did. She wouldn't be alone anymore. She should have thought of getting a pet a long time ago.

"You're welcome," he said gruffly. "I wanted to get you something that was as special as the train you gave me. I can't thank you enough for that."

"It was nothing. I knew it was the one thing you'd never buy for yourself."

She got the dog settled with her bowls of food and water and then took off her snow boots and the gloves and set them on the counter.

"So, Santa, before this goes any further, why are you here? Is it just for tonight?" she asked.

"No. I'm here because I love you, Penny. From the moment I walked away from you, every instinct I had was telling me to turn around and go back to you. But I was too afraid to do that. I wasn't sure I could figure out how to live with my fears about you."

She stayed where she was, afraid to rush to the wrong conclusion. "And now you are?"

He stood up and walked over to her, still carrying his Santa bag. "Yes, Penny, I am. All day today I kept seeing you in my chalet and then I went outside and you were there, too. I don't think running back home is going to change the fact that you are in my heart now, Penny. I don't want to live without you."

She watched him, trying not to get too excited, but she couldn't help it. "So what do you want to do about this?"

"What you suggested," he said. "Let's figure out how to bring our lives together. Date each other and figure out if this love is something that will last. That is, if you even still love me."

She shook her head. "Of course I still love you! I was mad at you for walking out, but it takes a long time to fall out of love. That is why I've always been afraid to let myself care about a man. A man like you who has everything I wanted but never knew I was looking for." Suddenly, she gave him an apprehensive look. "But before we go any further, Will, I need to know one thing."

"What?" he asked.

"Are you sure about this?"

He took a step closer to her, smiled broadly and framed her face in his large hands. "More sure than I've been of anything in my life."

Then he reached into his bag and took out a sprig of mistletoe and held it over her head.

"Really?"

"Wasn't sure you'd let me kiss you without it," he said.

She took a deep breath. Then threw herself at him, knocking his Santa's hat off his head, and his bag fell to the ground as he caught her. Their mouths met and they kissed. The embrace was long and fierce and they both whispered each other's names and promises they meant to keep.

He carried her to the sofa and made love to her in the reflection of the light from the fireplace and the brilliantly lit Christmas tree. She held him as close to her as she could.

He cradled her to his chest and stroked his hand up

and down her back. "I was so afraid that I'd done too good of a job convincing you that I didn't need you in my life, when the opposite was true. I've never been good at admitting I needed anyone. But I don't think I can live without you, Penny."

She leaned up on her elbow, resting it against his chest, and looked down into his face so dear to her, with those beautiful blue eyes. "I need you, too. You were right—I was afraid that I'd fallen for a guy who wouldn't love me again. I think I was projecting my fears on you—"

"While I was doing the same to you. But we're together now and we will be for good."

"Yes, for good." She gave him an inquisitive look. "Um…where do you live?"

"California."

"I wondered after you got me that job interview out there. I guess you were trying to make sure you'd see me again."

"I guess I was," he admitted ruefully. "I can't imagine my life without you."

He pulled her into his arms, bringing his mouth down on hers, and she felt as if she'd had the best Christmas ever. Will was the present she'd always wanted but never dreamed of having.

* * * * *

*Ring in the New Year with AFTER MIDNIGHT (January 2015), the final chapter in the* HOLIDAY HEAT *miniseries.*
*When Lindsey Collins and Carter Shaw finally give in to the sexual tension between them, there will definitely be fireworks!*

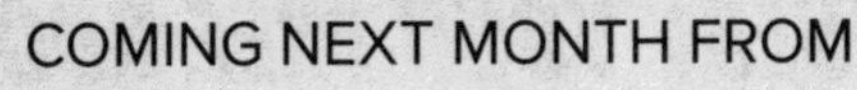

Available December 16, 2014

## #827 SEDUCING THE MARINE

*Uniformly Hot!*

by Kate Hoffmann

Marine Will McIntyre wants two things—to get back to his unit after an injury, and Dr. Olivia Eklund. Olivia is very tempted, but she knows the sooner Will heals, the sooner he'll leave her...

## #828 WOUND UP

*Pleasure Before Business*

by Kelli Ireland

After one mind-blowing night with Grace Cooper, Justin Maxwell demands more from his former student. But Grace has big plans for her future, and every moment with Justin puts that future at risk...

## #829 HOT AND BOTHERED

by Serena Bell

Cleaning up an infamous guitarist's reputation shouldn't be that hard for image consultant Haven Hoyt. But once she gets her hands on Mark Webster, neither can resist their attraction—or the temptation never to let go!

## #830 AFTER MIDNIGHT

*Holiday Heat*

by Katherine Garbera

It's New Year's Eve and überserious skier Lindsey Collins resolves to have a sexy fling. But bad-boy snowboarder Carter Shaw is determined to show her he's more than a good time.

---

He was hungry, desperate, and Olivia surrendered to the overwhelming assault. Will pulled her close and then, as if he were uncertain, held her away. But their lips never broke contact. Frustrated by his indecision, she furrowed her fingers through his tousled hair and tightened her grip, refusing to let him go.

"Tell me what you want," he whispered, his lips pressed against the curve of her neck.

Olivia knew exactly what she wanted. She wanted to tear her clothes off, finish undressing Will, then drag him to the nearest bed. She wanted to spend the day discovering all the things she didn't know about him and all the things she'd forgotten. Most of all, she wanted to lose herself in sexual desire.

This wasn't love, she told herself. It was just pure, raw desire...





HBEXP79831

# Love the Harlequin book you just read?

Your opinion matters.

Review this book on your favorite book site, review site, blog or your own social media properties and share your opinion with other readers!

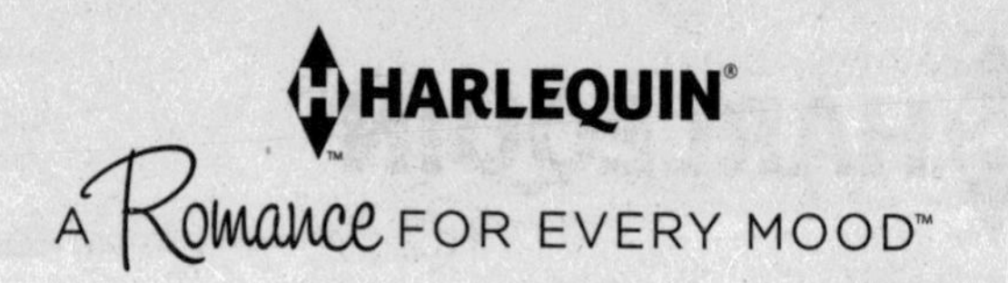


# JUST CAN'T GET ENOUGH?

Join our social communities
and talk to us online.

You will have access to the latest news on upcoming titles and special promotions, but most importantly, you can talk to other fans about your favorite Harlequin reads.

Harlequin.com/Community

Facebook.com/HarlequinBooks

Twitter.com/HarlequinBooks

Pinterest.com/HarlequinBooks

HSOCIAL

HARLEQUIN®
A Romance FOR EVERY MOOD™